Ink

The Written Trilogy: Book One

Vika Grace

Plaid With Stripes Publishing

Copyright © 2015 by Plaid with Stripes Publishing

Plaid With Stripes Publishing paperback edition 2015

Made is the USA

ISBN: 978-1-329-06405-8

For Nick, the Storymaster

For Ben, the one who's gonna pay my bills when I'm a
starving artist

For Allie, ma soeur et mon amie

Chapter 1

Running.

Running.

Branches clawed at my face. I stumbled over and over on the roots webbing the forest floor.

They had gone too far this time.

My footfalls were heard for miles around, I was sure of that much.

I ran from *them.*

My thoughts fled in one direction. I didn't know where I was going at first, but piece by piece my scattered thoughts jammed back together and a single place filled my imagination.

I fled through the lonely nights and days, resting only when every last speck of energy had drained from the very fibers of my being and I couldn't push myself to take one more step. The only possessions I had with me were the clothes on my back, and father's leather bracelet strapped around my wrist where it always was. He supposedly said it brought him luck, but I wouldn't know, I was two when he died. My mother told he was some kind of hero from the Ancient Orc tribes. He died in the Great Battle when Nyverden got their freedom from Worglo.

My muscles screamed for rest. I fell at the bank of a little pond in the middle of a break in the trees and drank greedily from the murky waters. I pulled my face up from the surface, choking on the earthy water running down my throat. The water shook, ripples from the drops rolling off my face echoing out and then disappearing at the edge of the bank. Eventually the water stilled, reflecting my own face back at me.

Streaks of sweat ran down my sage-stained skin. Long, pointed ears, short, jutting tusks. I glared at the face in the water. I could never go back. Nobody wanted me there. The feeling was mutual.

My mother was the only exception. She was one of those people who always gave off this kind of light that made even the world seem a little nicer. We looked nothing alike, despite our blood, so no one would believe she was my mother unless they knew us and our story.

Time passed in the moments of when I ate and when I slept. It had nothing to do with the actual suns and moons that rose or fell. Growing up in the forest with a healer for a mother, I knew which plants to eat and to avoid, but it wasn't long before the trees thinned out and I reached the massive stone walls that encircled the city. I had only ever heard about it. Lost in the wonderful unfamiliar ness of those walls, I followed the sea of people from the carriage road towards the city gate. I immediately became very aware that I looked more like a wild animal and less like the "civilized" son of a healer. But really though, growing up in the wild with an orc Tribe, how civilized was I expected to be? Even if my mother was an elf. My massive feet were caked with a dark mix of mud and blood from the wild paths, my clothes coated with the same. The gray wall loomed over me, replacing the trees that used to fill my horizon.

  Walking in the crowd involved more sorry's, and excuse me sir's than I would've thought. I got jostled around by the people rushing off to somewhere or nowhere, and yelled at more than once in more than one language. I spoke Kaelic, the most common language in the known world, and Orcish, thanks to living so close to the Tribe, even a little Elven, so I thought I knew languages. Apparently not. I towered over most of the crowd of humans, half elves, and maybe a couple of full elves pushing through the torrent of people. Over the sea of heads, my eyes met with an orc and we gave each other a nod before he could see what I really was. To the untrained eye, I was just a smaller, slimmer orc. If someone looked closer though, they'd see I actually look more like a tall, green elf with tusks. Usually that realization comes with people throwing up in their mouths.

  Elves and orcs don't mix.

  They just don't.

  The crowd pulled me through the yawning city gates and into the chaos of the marketplace. Every language under the sun was being screamed at the top of everyone's lungs. Shatterpoole was mostly known for its magnificent crime and corrupt aristocracy. The city was laid out in rings- the deeper into the center of the city you go, the cleaner the area gets. Well, the crime is cleaner; you're more likely to be poisoned by a political "ally" than ripped apart by some ill-mannered bum off the street who thought you looked particularly threatening. The city was technically ruled by the Ducrast family. How they got to power is somewhat of a mystery, and will probably remain that way as long as they have it. The family that you really didn't want to mess with was the Antimarx, an old blue blood family of warlocks (which means one of their ancestors was a demon, and one can only assume how that affects their personalities) who have a notorious reputation for running the drug trade that ruled the city. The Ducrasts may have the official rule, but Stein Antimarx ran this town.

I entered the city through the east side of the outer ring, which was not the nicest part of town by any means. The streets looked like they may have been cobblestone at one point, but time and use had crumbled them beyond carriage-worthy. The buildings were less than stable wooden structures with ragged curtains hanging over the windows to keep out curious stares. People bustled around me hurrying off to get home before dinner. I staggered in the middle of the crowd, ignoring my exhaustion from running through the woods like a madman for the past few days, taking in all the excitement of the city.

"Excuse me, sir," I turned myself around to see a girl with a shocking mess of dark orange hair falling in wild waves down to her waist. I wasn't sure to be more surprised by her hair, or by the fact that someone just called me "sir".

"Hi?" I wasn't really sure what else to say.

"I was wondering if I could read your palm for you, I have a talent for it," she added an innocent grin to that last sentence. If the stories taught me anything about Shatterpoole, nobody's innocent here. Ignoring my better judgment, I stretched out my massive hand to her.

"Hmmm, it's difficult to say," she concentrated intently with her cool green eyes. "Oh, yes, I see, you have a lot of trouble ahead of you." I could've guessed as much.

She pushed back her wild hair, gave me that pretty smile, patted my hand, and ran off into the shadows.

Oh yes, very talented.

I looked down at my hand and noticed instantly that the little rat had somehow slipped my father's bracelet off my wrist. Innocent girl? I think not.

"Hey! Hold on!" I sprinted in the direction I thought I saw her go. The fading light was no bother to me at all, considering I can see perfectly in the dark. My legs were already lead, and my feet were like bricks. A person can only run so much. *"Where are you?!"* I let out a monstrous roar. The one thing I had left of him was gone. I was really killing this city-thing so far.

Ignoring my exhaustion from the past few days in the woods, I sprinted in and out of alleys, up and down streets, and tore through the swarming marketplace with no luck. After about two hours of running through the lower rings of the city, my final bits of energy was gone. Even if I had found her at that point, I would've been too tired to do much else. I slumped down in an alleyway falling asleep with the sounds of glass shattering and screaming ringing in this distance.

Welcome to Shatterpoole.

Something was crawling on top of me. Shooting up into sitting position, an unsuspecting stray cat a few feet across the littered alleyway. Startled, I mumbled a quick apology and scrambled to my feet. I brushed the grimy straw off me, and walked toward the edge of the alley. My stomach growled and my throat felt like old sandpaper. Brooding at the edge of the alley, I scanned the street, reviewing my options. My stomach gave me another growl.

Not even a day in the city and I'm already getting robbed. And by a girl.

I rubbed my bare wrist where the leather band used to be.

The first rays of morning were still chasing away the fog. Despite the early hour, there was a crowd of the rag-tag citizens going about their morning business. The cleaner looking ones looked like craftsmen or maids going off to serve in shops or the manors in the inner rings. Most of them, though, looked like they were headed over to the docks that made this port city famous. Most of them, though, had that dull stare in their eyes like there was a body but nothing inside. Rushing over the cracked road, hundreds of creatures of every variety passed by. A human girl with embody black curls passed by carrying a basket of steaming rolls, making me drool just a little.

I needed to find something to eat, drink, preferably both.

I had been used to drawing offended stares before. My very existence disturbed most people. Here though, nobody seemed to really care what I was. It was nice. Sliding into the flow of the crowd, I headed in the direction that seemed to be where most of them were going, hoping to catch up with that girl with the bread. More than once I bumped into an unsuspecting peddler and even knocked over an entire table of cheap-looking medallions and charms that a very aggressive Halfling had been trying a little too hard to sell. After the Halfling had nearly screamed my ear off with his high-pitched laments about his overturned table, I lost the bread girl, but found a tavern with a large blue bear dancing on the sign that swung above the door. I'm not really sure why, but the bear caught my attention, and I decided to walk inside and see what they had for food. I had no money, but I was hoping I could work for something.

It being only the early morning, few were at the bar, and a handful of people were occupying the tables scattered around the large room. They were all humans, each looked very drawn in themselves with glazed over stares that early mornings usually included. Only a few of them bothered to look up when I came in and rang the bell at the edge of the long bar. The faded purple curtain pulled back to reveal a girl around my age with flaming dark orange waves falling around her face-

Her.

The street rat who stole my father's bracelet.

Eyes wide with horror, she spun around and ducked back behind the curtain.

"Hey!" I climbed over the bar and scrambled after her. Behind the curtain I found a dark kitchen with a redhead dominating the center of it and brandishing a frying pan.

Threat sparked in her eyes.

"Stay back," I saw her knuckles turn white gripping her improvised weapon.

"Give back what you stole." I rose to my full six foot four inches and took a step forward. She didn't move. "Look, just give it back and I'll leave you alone." She lowered the pan a little. Her big green eyes locked with mine.

"I'm not going to hurt you," I hesitated to say the next thing because it sounded petty even in my head- "just give me my bracelet back."

"I don't have it." She watched me curiously with those big eyes, frying pan shielding part of her face.

I sucked in a deep breath of air to fight the urge to lose my cool. There was a long moment where I was mentally counting backwards from ten. I wanted my piece of home back. My piece of him.

I was about to let go of my hard-fought calm when she threw her hands up.

"They were gonna kill you! What did you want me to do? Stand back and *watch*? Although, I'm regretting it now."

"What are you talking about?!" This girl wasn't a just thief, she was nuts.

"You wouldn't believe me if I told you."

"Try me." I thought of myself as a pretty open-minded kind of guy. I was a half orc half elf for heaven's sake.

"How special is that thing anyways? The only value it could possibly have would have to be sentimental."

"I will rip your fingers off one at a time if you don't cough it up right now."

"Now, now," she waved a delicate hand. "No need for unnecessary violence-"

"Says the girl who was ready to hit me with a freaking frying pan a minute ago." She either tells me what the heck is going on, or she doesn't.

"What would *you* do if a giant orc was coming after you?"

I hesitated. "*Half* orc." Half monster.

"Oh." I looked down at her with the dark blue, elven eyes- the punchline of a thousand jokes back home. "Fine. I'll tell you, but it's going to sound weird.

"I can handle it," I said.

"You have been warned." Her bright eyes flicked up at me before she continued. "I didn't lie to you yesterday when I said I'm good at telling fortunes. I'm an *aspicien*."

"A *what*?" Yes, this girl was insane.

"Oh come on, do you live in a hole? An aspicien? A person who can see into someone's past, present, and future? Tell me you've at least heard of them."

"Sorry to disappoint." I literally had no idea what she was talking about. The only magic I had seen was healing spells from my mother.

"I saw you getting killed over your stupid bracelet, so I took it."

"Um, thanks."

11

"You *should* be thanking me, I saved your miserable life." I narrowed my eyes at her.

"If it's so miserable, then why'd you save it?"

"That's none of your business," she defiantly lifted her sharp chin into the air between us. "Besides, if I had taken the time to explain all this to you, you would've been dead by now, so, you're welcome." I sighed at her angrily. "I'll give you your silly bracelet back."

I put my hand out to take it, trying not to hate her for this whole thing.

She just looked at me for a good second. "I gave to a friend to hold on to. I can get it by tomorrow." Why she'd give such a worthless thing to a friend to hold onto anyways? Against my better judgment I demanded to go with her so I'd be sure she wouldn't cross me again, and to see what she was up to.

"We got off on the wrong foot-"

"No kidding." Robbing people is no way to make friends.

"No, really," she said, hardly skipping a beat. "I think we should be friends. You're clearly new here and I need someone of your, um, size, on my side."

I looked at her indignantly.

"Oh for heaven's sake, my name's Aengel." She stuck out her hand for me to shake. This was a human custom that I was aware of but never participated in. She must've noticed my hesitation. "It's a hand. You shake it, but don't crush it." Slowly I put my hand out and lightly closed it around hers to move it up and down. She gave a small laugh, not an unkind one like the sort I was used to. "It's okay, we'll work on it." She pulled her hand away and tilted her sharp chin up to look at me in the eyes. She only came up to about my chest. "What's your name?"

I shrugged. "I'm in between names." I ran away before the Elders gave me my adult name.

"So, then what was the last one you had?"

"You don't want to know," I grimaced at the memory.

"Well I have to call you *something*." She pushed back her temperamental hair and looked around the dark kitchen for inspiration. Then she studied my face for long moment. I folded my arms.

"How about your father's name?"

"Krill?"

"Like the little fish?" She looked mildly amused for half a second and seemed like she might've even laughed.

Well, that *name won't do.*

My stomach growled, reminding me of the reason I came in here in the first place. Being in a kitchen wasn't really helping either.

"I don't really care what you call me at this point," I said. "Just as long as you have something for me to eat."

"Well, I can't have you starving to death." She disappeared into the little store room that was tucked in the corner of the dark kitchen. "Make yourself at home," she called out. "Go sit at the bar or something." I sighed and trudged out to the big dining room at the front of the tavern that I had first entered, wondering if I had made a serious mistake trusting this girl.

Chapter 2

Aengel insisted we couldn't go and find her friend until nightfall, which I found extremely suspicious. Then again, everyone around here was suspicious. I couldn't shake the feeling that I shouldn't be trusting her. She gave me food though, so that had to count for something. At least I wasn't aimlessly wandering around the streets like the day before. Until the sun set, she put me to use out back chopping firewood and then I had the *honor* of moving the new bedframes up the tavern stairs to the rooms that travelers rent during their stays here in the outer ring. Whatever she needed more for, it usually included heavy lifting.

Racist.

The story goes she was the adopted daughter of the man who owned the tavern, who was also the cook. It was just them two and one other barmaid in her late teens running the place.

As the day wore on, the dining room started to fill up and come to life. Weary lowerclassmen poured in off the streets in search of something to warm their bones and drown their day before it even really began. Road-worn travelers filled the rooms for rent upstairs and sat at the tables by the fireplace exchanging stories. I wanted more than anything to listen, but Aengel had me running around most of the day working on this or that. A skinny, red faced man who looked like he had witnessed creation first hand was in the kitchen when I went through, moving firewood from back into the dining room. He was struggling under a wicker basket overflowing with all kinds of vegetables.

I dropped the wood and rushed over to help him, legitimately afraid of the basket crushing him.

"Ooh what a gentleman, yes, yes. A gentleman. Very rare these days among the youth. Oh very rare." He patted my scared arm sweetly and hobbled over to the basket and picked out a bunch of carrots. I did my best not to be too weirded out. Old people always made me nervous for some reason. My guess is that all the Elders back the Tribe practically throwing up every time they saw me didn't help. I placed the basket on the counter and turned to get back to moving the wood.

"Oh, young man!" He called out. "Could I steal you for a moment?" I nodded. "Would you be a good lad and reach some pots for me. I usually have Aengel do it, but since you're here, might as well not. I hate having her climb up the cabinets, most unlady-like." I just nodded, not really sure what to say.

"You're not really much for conversation, are you?"

"Not really."

"Ah, so you *can* speak." I nodded. Slowly. "Oh good, I was beginning to think you were one of those mute fellows." Then he went on about some lad he had known years before who could only make animal sounds.

"Is he bothering you?" I turned around to see Aengel with arms folded, but a smile on her face.

"No, not really," I gave the best version of a sweet smile that one with tusks can muster.

The old man grinned back. "We were just having a chat."

He put down the knife he had been using to cut up the carrots and wiped his bony hands on his apron. "I've been so rude, I'm Sal." I did better on my handshaking this time, and Aengel noted it with a hint of satisfaction flickering on her face. "What am I supposed to call you, laddie?" I shrugged. Aengel grabbed a strand of her hair and told the old man I didn't have a name. It was slightly true, but her casual words still stung somewhere in my half monster heart. I thought of Brother Elijah. He was an old priest, my friend in the years before old age took him. He was our supplier for the herbs my mother used in her healing trade. He was a Catholic priest who lived in a solitary hut beside his precious herb garden. In the days before he fell ill of the Consumption, I would go over there to pick up herbs, but would end up sitting in the garden with the old man for hours on end.

"You could call me Eli."

Aengel was looking me, I suddenly realized. Not just looking, but really *looking*, as it she actually saw something worth looking at.

"Yeah, that's suits you."

"It's settled then," Sal announced. Turning to me he added, "Welcome to the family, Eli my boy."

Eli.

I glowed somewhere deep down.

"Now off to work, both of you!" Sal half-heartedly waved his butcher knife at us. I almost had time to wonder what kind of work exactly Aengel had in mind for me after I had finished with the wood. Almost. She didn't waste a breath rattling off a list of various odd jobs she needed done before disappearing off to serve the guests in the dining room.

I was so absorbed in sanding the new bed frames an hour later that I noticed the night falling when the colors of the room began to fade. Seeing in the dark has its perks, but I can't see colors. That means no midnight painting, which is fine because I don't paint anyways. I heard a loud knocking on the worn door of the shed I was using for a workshop.

"Yeah?"

"I've been looking all over for you," Aengel glided through the door and sat herself on one of the unfinished chairs someone assembled years ago, but apparently didn't bother to finish. "Better finish up, Sir Carpenter- we've got things to do." I stood up and grimacing when I stretched out my legs. I didn't notice them cramping up while I was on my knees sanding. She looked at me up and down. "You need to change."

I laughed, "I doubt you'd find anything that could fit me."

"Don't be so full of yourself." She brushed past me to inspect my work. "Nice," I heard her mutter.

"Why?" I looking down at my worn pants and dirty white (well, it *was* white) shirt my mother made for me before I tore the sleeves off. Well, they got ripped off by someone else. In a fight.

I said my Tribe hated me.

"My friend is kind of a snob. Plus, you stink." Ow. "It's still pretty early, so you have time to wash up and get some new clothes on." She started making her way past me to the door again. "I got you some things, no need to thank me, it was Sal's idea. Your room is at the end of the hallway to the left upstairs."

"Thanks, anyways." Always be polite. That's what my mother taught me.

"No problem." I thought I saw her blush. "So," she watched me finish sanding the final frame for a minute. "Where you from?"

I looked up for a second. "The woods."

"Why'd you leave?"

"Why not?" She didn't need to know the truth.

Carefully, I put away the tools Sal lent me and closed up the shed before heading into the back door of the tavern.

"Oh come on, I can tell what you are. Is that why you left?"

I turned to face her, big eyes staring up at me, taking in my every word like they were all she cared about. "You ask a lot of questions."

She shrugged and told me to hurry up and get ready before disappearing out the door.

17

I gave the old cook a quick greeting when I went through the kitchen into the main room that was bursting with the noise of the growing crowd, and then up the stairs to the rooms that are usually reserved for travelers. I easily located mine with the door unlocked. I pushed it open to find a good-sized bedroom with a single bed under a window that looked like the soft linen quilt had been carefully tucked around the mattress. There was a table on the far wall and a chair sitting beside it. On the table I noticed a package with 3 letters scrolled across the paper in big, loopy letters.

"Eli". Me.

I gently picked up the parcel and gingerly peeled the paper away. Inside was a used, but still new-looking, pair of black pants and a wine colored tunic that had black chord criss crossing up from the middle of my chest. I don't think I've ever owned clothes like these. It did occur to me that they were probably stolen, but if the boot fits... I hadn't noticed a door on the left wall, but when I opened it, it revealed a large wooden tub in the center of a tiny room with a little mirror one of the walls on top of a wooden shelf with a lump of soap stuck to it.

It took me longer than I expected to get ready. Wanting to make sure I was up to standard with the clothes I'd be wearing, I spent an exceptional amount of time scrubbing every inch of my dark green skin. Maybe I was subconsciously trying to wash the color out. After I was satisfied with myself, and sufficiently smelled like the pine scented soap, I began to work on what to do about my hair. Wiry and jet black, it was notorious for disobeying orders. I had given up long ago trying to do much about it, and kept the sides short and the rest longer. It stuck up as if I had been struck by lightning, giving me an even wilder look than my green skin and tusks would on their own. After running through the forest for the past few days, I was getting a savage looking beard.

The perks of being half orc.

I was making the finishing touches on my appearance when furious knocking shook my door.

"Eli! What on *earth* are you doing in there?" I was still getting used to the name, so it took a second for me to realize the voice was talking to me in particular. Somehow it was already completely dark outside and the moon was halfway up the sky.

"Sorry!" I threw open the door. Aengel stood in the hallway, wearing a deep green linen kirtle with a cream colored underdress showing through the loosely crossed chord that secured the green layer around her. Against the green, her fiery red hair blazed with color, wildly tumbling down her back and her light eyes glinted at me. I must've been wearing my thoughts on my face, because she snickered and said:

"Pick up your jaw, half-orc, and lets go." I gave a nervous laugh and followed her down the stairs and out the door into the chilled autumn night.

Chapter 3

The streets of the city were just as busy as they were this afternoon, but the people were less coordinated. Artfully, the two of us weaved through the crowd toward the outer edge of the city and towards this friend of hers. People managed to knock into one of us every 100 feet. I would like to think that was because the streets were narrow and crowded.

Even though I'm not familiar with Shatterpoole, even remotely, I could tell we were moving out from the center to the docks. The crowded got bigger and more aggressive in their walking. The houses became more like shacks pieced together with scrap wood and rags rather than actual buildings. By the time we got into the official slums, Aengel was walking so close to me, I could feel her hair brushing against my arm. I was *more* than concerned I had made a mistake following her here. A bony old man with no eyes ran in front of us, nearly knocking her down. I grabbed her arm to steady her, and she gave me a look of nervous gratitude I knew she was too proud to admit.

Skeletons with sunken, dead eyes lined the streets and watched us from the banks of trash on the edge of the road. The crowd began to thin out as we reached the end of the city. I didn't know it, but we had made our way to the slum docks, not the docks they use for most of the trade. It was the heart of all shady activity in Shatterpoole. The reason the crowd had been thinning out was partly because it was the edge of the city, the other part was because even the beggars avoided this part of town.

"What?"

"Don't look now, but we're being followed," she whispered up to me.

"Why am I not surprised?" That earned me a sideways glare. "Hey, are we almost there? Not that I don't love a midnight stroll, but I'd like to have some idea of where we're going."

"We're looking for a ship called *La Tortue Portal,* that's where my friend is who has your bracelet."

"Your friend a sailor?"

"No, she's just on a ship."

"Does she live on it?"

"*Saints alive,* I don't know." She gave me a playful whack on the arm failing to hide her obvious anxiety. The slum docks was probably the worst place to be at night. A scream shattered in the distance. Under the yellow light of the full harvest moon, I saw her face go pale and body jolt.

"Aengel?" I grabbed her shoulders and watched as her eyes grew wild and unfocused. "Aengel? What's happening?!" As quickly as it came on, her pupils retracted to their normal size and the color flushed back into her face. She gave me a startled look.

"Problem?" She threw her gaze away and shrugged my hands off her shoulders.

"Well yeah, you just kind of had a *moment.*"

"I didn't know you met an elf," she mumbled to herself, as if that explained why she almost gave me a heart attack.

"Did you just use your crazy prophet powers on me!?" I stepped away from her.

"I can't control it! It just happens sometimes. I'm not used to touching people. I shouldn't have whacked you." The lamps made her face look more red than it already was. I guess a whack on the arm counted as touching.

I tried to shrug it off like it was no big deal, but it kind of was. It was weird that she knew things about me when we only knew each other for less than 24 hours.

"Keep walking, we're almost there," she plowed ahead of me and kept her distance from then on. Out of the corner of my eye, I saw a shadow move across one of the shacks. It almost looked human, but I didn't really get a good look at it. Hoping it was just a trick of the light, I turned away to catch up with the redhead.

Finally, we came upon an abandoned looking ship with barely legible letters carved on the side spelling out "*La Tortue Poral*". She led the way up the ramp onto the empty deck.

I shivered.

In vain, I tried to keep the ramp steady while I climbed up. Aengel stood on the deck of the ship, watching me struggling up with more than a hint of amusement.

"Ever been on a boat before?"

I heaved myself on deck, letting out a sigh of relief before the waves started rocking us again.

"Nope." I pitched forward, barely catching myself before I almost crashed into Aengel. "How do you *not* fall over?" She seemed perfectly at home on the waves.

"You get used to it," she said. "Don't worry."

The ship seemed ancient enough to be haunted. I prayed that wasn't the case. From the main deck we went through a door so small that I had to duck down so I wouldn't slam my face into the rotten wood. Aengel cheering me on while I inched along. From there we climbed down a flight of stairs that were so old, Sal had probably seen them in their prime, and then we came to another door after that. The farther down we went, the stronger this perfumed smell attacked my nose. The door at the bottom of the steps was closed, but I could see light pouring out from in between the door and its frame. Aengel knocked a particular rhythm in the center of the splintering boards. It swung open giving us a burst of the flowery scent. Inside was a large room, crammed with various odd-looking artifacts. There was a desk covered with scientific instruments and papers in the middle of the room, and then an ornate, red door on the far side of the mess. We picked our way across the room, trying not to bump into anything, and Aengel gave a loud knock. I heard a female voice call out from the other side.

"Enter!"

Aengel pushed open the heavy red door and closed it tightly behind me once I stepped into the small room. It consisted of a large desk and a large leather chair with a young woman sitting on it. She had raven black hair and electric blue eyes that were heavily made up with black rimming the edges. She wore black leather from head to toe, a cold smile hinted on her blood red lips. The air around her made me nervous for some reason. She radiated power and class. I saw why Aengel made me dress up.

"Aengel, what are you doing here?" she looked almost happy to see us, but not quite.

"I need that bracelet back. Remember the one I gave you last night?"

"Do I look ill? Of course I remember. I'm Czara, by the way." She stood up and strode over to the wall. Casually pulling away one of the boards to reveal a hidden cabinet. "I did what you asked, and it's actually a pretty interesting story." Then she looked at me as if seeing me for the first time. "Is this him?"

"I'm Eli," I stated. "If that's the 'him' you're asking about."

"It is," she turned back to the cabinet. She pulled out my worn, black leather bracelet that had caused me all this trouble. *Lucky bracelet indeed. The same luck that got my father killed.* She studied it for a moment with her virulent eyes, and then walked over to hand it back to me. I secured it around my wrist once again, and felt an immediate rush of relief. My piece of home was back where it belonged.

"So, do you want me to tell you what I found out? Or should I wait for *him* to leave?" Czara raised a dark eyebrow.

"Well, now you have to tell me, you can't just say something like that and expect me not want to know."

She gave me a look with her icy eyes. "I just did."

Aengel put her hands up and said that I should hear whatever Czara was about to say because it was, after all, my bracelet.

"The first thing you should know, half-orc, is that I'm a nidoren and a warlock. You look confused. Of course you do, you have no clue what that is. In fact, judging by what *I* know, it looks like *you've* been pretty well sheltered from life outside the tribe." She paused to admire my seething glare.

"Just so you know, a nidoren is someone who can touch an object and see what it has gone through. The untrained niddie, that's the slang term if you were wondering, sunshine, can only see about a week into the past. A trained one can see up to a year back." She gave us a cold smile. "I can see back 20."

I tried to look indignant.

"Aengel lent me your bracelet after she saw someone kill you over it in a vision so I could find out why one would kill over such a worthless-"

"It's not *worthless.*" I growled.

"To everyone else it is. And don't interrupt, it's rude. As I was saying, Aengel brought it here for me to get some information on. I skimmed the past 20 years of that bracelet's existence until I found something interesting." She gave me a mocked knowing look. "And did I ever."

She knew too much.

"The bracelet is a souvenir from your father's glory days in the bounty hunting business." I saw Aengel give me a sideways look and the warlock continued with her report. "Your father was part of a bounty hunting agency in

24

Shatterpoole, actually, and this proved his identification to other hunters. The seal of the moon stamped on the middle of the band is the logo. Interestingly enough, daddy made some choices that made the head of the agency *uncomfortable*. He killed an Antimarx, one of the most powerful families in Shatterpoole even though it wasn't an assignment. Actually, he was specifically told *not* to kill this one. Your mother helped him too. They were part of the same bounty-hunter team with three others. Each of them had their own reason to kill Carvel Antimarx, Stein's favorite son and heir. The two elves in the group hated him because he started the Great Fire that burned down a considerable amount of elven forests so he could build another estate."

She counted them on her pale fingers. "I'm not really sure why the two humans hated him, but in any case, they were both out for blood. Your father wanted him dead because Carvel was about to launch a genocide against the orcs. He had only come by that information because of an aspicien, by the way. The five of them killed one of the most powerful men in the entire known world. They might've gotten away with it too, if Carvel wasn't a warlock or an Antimarx. One of the humans died, and the rest escaped just to be hunted the rest of their lives.

Since then, daddy is the only other one the Antimarx got to. The three remaining members are living in hiding or are still adventuring and don't care that a demon-blooded family of madmen are after them. Don't worry, I don't think they know about you. Nobody seemed to know your father and one of the elves had a thing going, and nobody would even imagine them having any kind of *offspring*." Her face didn't soften. "Actually, the fact that your kind is so inconceivable is probably what has protected you all these years."

Wow. That was a lot to take in. I stood there for a moment and Aengel and I just stared at Czara as we tried to process it all. Talk about an information-dump.

"Well, now what do we do?" I said, running a hand through my hair.

"First you're going to pay me," Czara began. "And then you're going to pray to whatever god, saint, or higher power that you believe in that the Antimarxs haven't noticed you in the city and revived their campaign against your parents' old team. Because if they did, consider yourself royally screwed."

"I think they already found us," Aengel pointed out. "We were being followed on the way here."

"And why, pray tell, did you lead them here?" Czara calmly sat back down in her big leather chair behind the desk.

"I think we lost him before we got on the ship."

"'I think' is not good enough. If you get killed walking home tonight, it'll be your own damn fault. If you don't get killed and they find my hideout, I'll do the Antimarxs a favor." Her face was emotionless. "After you pay me, of course."

"I thought we were partners," she pulled out a little drawstring bag from her pocket hidden in the seam of her skirt and fished out two gold coins. Warlocks were expensive, partners or not. I should've known better- Czara didn't look like the type to give out favors.

We left then, and somehow made it back to the Blue Bear Tavern alive. Of course, inwardly we jumped at every shadow that shifted and every sound of life that rang out in the almost-empty early hour streets of the city. Once we got back to the tavern I walked Aengel to her room out of some unspoken agreement, and we said a quick good night. I was almost certain she could hear my heart palpitating. Whoever was following us earlier though, had clearly disappeared. When I got to my own room, I peeled off my new clothes that were now soaked in sweat despite the October chill, and dove into my bed. It was surprisingly comfortable and the quilt smelled of lavender. Exhaustion from the day washed over me the second my head hit the pillow and I was fast asleep before I could even snuggle down into the soft white sheets and think about what the warlock had just told me.

Chapter 4

The next day was a Sunday. The only reason I'd know that was because it was the sound of church bells that dragged me out of sleep. The first thing I noticed when I opened my eyes was how the white quilt fibers almost glowed in the late morning light, the second thing I noticed was that I was sprawled out on the wooden floor next to my bed with the quilt twisted around me.

Making a sounds reminiscent of my father's ethnic background, I untangled myself and threw on my old clothes before heading down the stairs into the big dining room. Aengel and the other barmaid were serving the less religious who were having their breakfasts while the pious were at which ever temple they served. Personally, I'd like to believe in the Christian god, but I wasn't human in any way, shape, or form, so His Grace did not extend to me as far as I knew. The orc race claims to have their own god, but he's not the kind I'd like to believe in. My elven mother's religion worships nature, protecting the natural world and vanquishing evil. I suppose that's why she was brave enough to kill one of the most powerful men in the known world- he sounded pretty evil according to Czara.

Aengel spotted me when I lumbered down the stairs and waved me over. She was wearing the light green kirtle that made her pale emerald eyes stand out.

"Good morning, sleeping beauty," she scolded. "I hope you're awake, because I have a long list for you today."

"Oh, joy." I took the folded piece of paper from her hand and turned to go the kitchen to see if Sal had anything for me.

"You *can* read, right?" She said before I had walked away.

"Of course I can," I called over my shoulder. "I'm smarter than I look."

"Whatever you say," she was smiling. I didn't even have to look back to see it, but I did.

After a quick breakfast with Sal, I started going through the list she made for me. That girl was a slave driver in another life. Distantly, I mused whether or not I'd be getting paid for any of this, although my room and board was probably more than enough payment. Less than a week away from home, and I already had two jobs: tavern maintenance man by day and bodyguard by night. The thing was, I still wasn't completely sure why Aengel really needed a bodyguard. She seemed safe enough here at the Bear. Then again, I had only known her for a couple days and had learned *very* little.

I was moving the wine barrels from the storeroom in the kitchen to behind the bar when two hooded figures walked into the tavern. Taking almost no notice of them, I kept on rolling the barrel until a boot stomped down on the top of it, stopping it from moving and stopping me from ignoring them. I raised my eyes to meet those of the stranger's and stood to my full height. Our few customers glanced up curiously from their half-empty drinks.

"Can I help you?" I would've added "ma'am", or "sir", but the hoods kept me from knowing which.

"I'm confident you can." oh, so they were men. Or, at least, the one with his boot on my barrel was. He threw back the hood, revealing a man, as I suspected, in his mid-twenties with dark soulless eyes and slicked black hair. "I'm looking for a pretty little girl with red hair, have you seen her?" Whatever this guy wanted with her, it couldn't have been good. I mean, that's just common sense and reading between the lines here. I'm not one for lying, but Aengel may have been one of my only friends at this point, and I never really had a surplus of those. And I was, after all, her bodyguard. Plus she was pretty.

Time to play stupid.

I looked at him blankly, having no intention of telling him much of anything.

His jaw tightened. "Where is the girl called Aengel?"

"Angels are in heaven. Sir."

The stranger sucked in a deep breath. Then backhanded me. Honestly though, I think it hurt him more than it hurt me because I was unmoved, with only my cheek stinging for proof that he ever hit me at all. I was actually pretty impressed he managed to reach me with that much force, I'm not exactly standard height. Realizing that he was trying to physically intimidate a half orc with only his bare hands, he drew a great sword from inside the cloak and placed the tip on my chest. It took every bit of courage I had not to tremble.

My hands shook.

I had to stand my ground. I had to protect her. She'd do the same for me; I knew because she'd already saved my life once before.

"This is your last chance, orc," he spat. "Tell me where the girl is." I looked at the sword and saw my reflection in the silver blade. Tusks, scars, blue eyes.

"*Half* orc."

As he drew back his sword to execute the fatal blow, I jumped away with the speed and grace I inherited from my mother. Our audience gasped in excitement as he artfully arced his sword towards me. He had thrown too much force into the swing to stop mid-strike, so Sir Tough Guy ended up falling over the barrel and landing on his pretty face. His partner, who also turned out to be a man of the same age with long dark hair that fell in jagged layers around his shoulders, did not draw a sword. He didn't need one. He stood calmly with a ball of fire blazing two inches above his outstretched hand.

Our spectators oooed and ahhed at the violet flame, too doped up to realize the danger.

"I think we're done here," Sir Flowing Hair gave me a cruel smile. The door of the tavern burst open, almost ripping it off of the hinges.

"Leave him alone, Veit." Dominating the threshold was an elf. Eyes the color of ice and hair as black as the darkest winter night, pointing a silver-tipped arrow at the man's head.

Mother.

Mother?

Veit, apparently that was his name, turned to face her. Clearly surrendering wasn't his style. The man who was on the ground had gotten to his feet now, and had his sword at the ready, eyes fixed on the elf. Despite the rather terrible situation, I was actually really glad to see her.

"Lia, it's been too long," sword-guy snickered. "You haven't aged a day." *Of course not, she's an elf.*

"Leave the boy alone, he hasn't done anything to you worth death."

"This impertinent creature is hardly a boy."

"How dare you," mother growled, the arrow was still trained on Veit's head. I looked from one to another, wondering what kind of history they had that would constitute a conversation like this.

"Come and make me, she-elf." She loosed the arrow, and opened the floodgates.

It was all a blur.

I could hear only my savage cries as I picked up the barrel and hurled is at the man with the sword. Veit had somehow dodged the arrow and now he and Ma were hurling magical balls of fire at each other. Personally, seeing my own mother being so viciously destructive was more terrifying than anything. The barrel had knocked the guy with the sword over there unconscious, so I turned to help out Mother with her fellow warlock "friend". They had successfully destroyed most of the main dining room, and the few customers that were there at that time of day had fled in terror, finally realizing they weren't safe on the sidelines.

I might have too, if this wasn't my mother on the line.

Screaming, I thundered towards Veit with the intention of ripping off his head. Not something I'd normally do, but the man was shooting balls of fire at the woman who raised me. I never got the chance. Sword-guy was, in fact, *not* unconscious. My thigh exploded with pain. I tumbled to the floor with a loud crash. Hot, dark blood poured out from the gash and my vision faded around the edges. I saw Aengel behind the bar with throwing knife aimed at the man who felled me. Despite the fact that I was about to pass out from the pain and blood loss, I managed to heave myself off the ground and rise to my full height. Sword-guy was advancing toward Aengel with a winning smile. She stood her ground, but I could tell she was terrified. The black around my vision began to close in as I staggered toward him. Mother and Veit were too involved in their own fight to notice me, and Sword-guy had his back to me, thinking I was out of play.

But I wasn't.

Gasping with pain and half-conscious, I came up behind him and grabbed him by the hair.

"You're done here," I growled in his ear. With my last ounce of strength, I lifted him up and then slammed him into the ground.

I'm not sure what happened after that because that's when I passed out.

Chapter 5

"Rabbit, can you hear me?" I felt a cool hand rest on my forehead. "Rabbit? I'm sorry. So sorry..." I opened my eyes and myself in my room at the tavern with a very concerned-looking elf kneeling by my head.

"Hi, Ma." She gave me a reassuring smile and smoothed back my hair.

"I'm glad you awake," she said softly. "You've been asleep longer than I thought you would be." I looked around and noticed that night had already fallen. I was unconscious almost all day. Aengel would be mad I didn't finish that list she gave me earlier. With some effort I pulled myself up into sitting position and noticed my leg had been completely healed. Throughout the Tribe, Mother had been the most renowned healer ever known. I shouldn't have been surprised, she's healed me more than once in the past after merciless beatings from my larger peers. When the herbs didn't work, she had her magic to fall back on.

"You're lucky you have such thick bones or he would've taken your leg off." She gave me a look that only a mother could give. I wasn't an abomination to her, I wasn't a monster. I was her beautiful baby boy. It didn't really matter how many times she told me this, I never could see how. She didn't see the green skin or the tusks or the wiry, animal hair. She saw me, just me.

"I'm sorry I ran away," I mumbled.

"Rab, I would tell you that nothing is impossible, but disappearing from an elf is an exception." It was nice to hear my old name again, even if it reminded me of the shame I was running from in the first place. There was no light in the room. Neither of us needed it. We could see each other perfectly fine without the help of any lamp or candle.

"How did you find me?"

"I'm a bounty hunter, my love, it's what I do," she patted my hand gently and rose to leave. "If you're feeling well enough, dinner is being served downstairs. There was some damage, but people can be generous when they feel needed, so it's in decent enough shape. The regulars couldn't bear to see this place closed because of a little disarray." She gave me a kiss on the cheek and left, closing the door gently behind her.

Worried about somehow undoing my mother's healing job, I was careful in pulling my clothes back on and wondered how exactly they got off. Even more curious was how exactly they managed to carry my dead weight up the stairs. I'm not a little person. Really though, even if she is my mother, it kind of weirds me out that she took my pants off. When I pulled them on, I realized why. They were stiff with dry blood and there was a gaping slash in the left thigh. Thank heaven for the clothes Aengel got me for our first meeting with Czara, or I'd be walking around with half a bloody pant leg on one side. I pulled the nice clothes on, noticing the thick scar that now wrapped around the side of my left thigh, and went down into the dining room. On my way down I bumped into Aengel, who was carrying a wooden tray of food up the stairs. Luckily I didn't knock into her, it looked like some very hot tea and soup she was transporting.

"Oh hey, you're up." She exclaimed once she realized it was me who had almost crashed into her.

"Yeah, well, you can't get rid of me that easy."

"Who said I was trying?" She smiled. "I was about to bring you this, but it looks like you'll be coming down after all."

"Oh no, if you went through all this trouble, I wouldn't want it to be for nothing," I said. "I'm not really crazy about crowded dining rooms anyways." Let's blame that one on living in isolation for the first sixteen years of my life.

She shrugged and pulled the tray away when I reached for it. She informed me that she was perfectly capable of carrying food up stairs and that I should be in bed anyways after the near death experience I'd just had. Then it was my turn to shrug as she followed me up the wooden steps. When we reached my room, she relinquished the tray and before turning to go back downstairs she said quietly:

"I didn't know the elf was your mother." She said. "I guess that makes you a half elf."

"Yeah, not that I really look like one though," I gave a pained laugh and she gave a sympathetic smile.

"I think the green skin and the tusks through people off. I can see it now though."

"Oh yeah?"

"Yeah," she said. "You have the eyes." At that she turned and disappeared down the stairs, leaving me standing outside my door alone.

Was I the only one who could only see the monster?

I suppose Aengel told Ma that I was eating in my room, because she joined me a little while later, also seeking solace from the noise of the tavern during happy hour. After living for 16 years in the forest, one gets used to the quiet. Of course, the Tribe made all kinds of noise, but we were settled a little ways away from them. We each finished our bowls of soup in silence. It seemed like our peaceful days in the woods were distant memories now, and the quiet days were over.

"How did my father die?" I said. I'm not really sure why I said it. It just kind of blurted out.

Mother blinked, I could tell she was slightly taken aback by my forward questioning.

"He was murdered, I've told you this before."

"Not the whole story." I sat down cross legged on my bed as she sat poised in the chair beside me.

"No, not the whole story," She breathed out a light sigh before continuing. "I wanted to wait until you were older to tell you. Now that you are, I see no more reason to keep if from you. Especially now that you're in Shatterpoole."

I readied myself for the truth.

"I don't know how much you've learned already, but here's what you should know: Your father and I worked together at a bounty hunting agency. We weren't always assigned together, but we usually were. I don't really want to brag, but he and I often worked together on the elite team, which was comprised of the most highly trained assassins. Your second cousin was also on the team, actually. Have I told you that you have a second cousin?"

I shrugged and shook my head. I'd never heard of any extended family.

"I suppose I wouldn't have. We were in hiding, and I didn't want to bring up anything that might give us away while you were still too young. The elite team assassinated someone they shouldn't have, and I'm not sorry for it. It's our duty to preserve the good in this world, and that man was the opposite of good."

"Carvel Antimarx?"

"So you have heard of him," she noted.

"A niddie told me the whole story," I responded coolly, as if I knew more than I really did. Honestly, I still had more questions than I was willing to admit.

"How do you know what a niddie is?"

"Ma, it's been a steep learning curve the moment I walked out of the forest."

She shook her head. "I know."

"But what happened after you killed Carvel, exactly? I mean, I know that one of the humans was killed and then my father was killed later, but what really happened?" It felt weird saying "my father", but I wasn't sure what else to call him.

"Giles. That was the human. His name was Giles. After the five of us killed Carvel, the four who survived were identified by a niddie, she was employed by the Antimarx-"

"The Antimarx have their own personal niddie?"

"Don't be too surprised," she said gravely. "That makes it very easy for them to find people who they're hunting. Thankfully nobody outside of the elite team knew about your father and me," her eyes became glassy, but an elf never cries. "Initially all of us carried on our profession on our own since the agency fired us. They were afraid of the Antimarx blaming them for the assassination. I had to go into hiding when I became pregnant." She looked at me with all the love in the fabric of the universe, but I could see in her eyes that grain of regret. The regret that falling in love with an enemy of her race led her to the life of hiding and fear. The regret of me.

"Your father died working as a mercenary when the Antimarx found him. It only took four arrows in his skull. I don't know how they found him, but they are more than capable of finding anyone. If I didn't think that was true I wouldn't have raised you in an orc tribe."

"That was the last place they'd look for an elf," I noted.

"Yes, it is."

"Well it worked, we're both alive." That was a plus, at least.

"For now," she brushed back a jet black strand of hair that had fallen over her eyes. "The warlock in the Tavern today who tried to kill you was Veit Antimarx,

Carvel's only living brother. The other was Wace, Carvel's right hand man."

"Oh." That would explain how they knew my mother. But it didn't really explain why they knew Aengel. "What were they doing here, though?"

"I'm sure I don't know," she replied. "They couldn't have been looking for you. Honestly I think they're still trying to figure out who you are. It's not every day you find a half-elf with your heritage."

"No kidding," I fidgeted with my bracelet. "They said they were looking for Aengel."

"It was probably drug trade business then. The Veit and Wace are two of the biggest drug lords in the city."

"Why am I not surprised?"

"You'll find that the Antimarx rule most of the city- underworld included." I wasn't really talking about them. "I'm going to my room, I suggest you get some sleep. Until the Antimarx find out, don't go about telling people you're my son- for your own protection. The less you're connected to me, the better. They've seen me now, so that means either we go into hiding again or we end this."

I looked at my mother standing there in full adventure gear, looking like she could conquer the world with a mere glance. I wondered how we were related. I may look very little like her, but we both have one thing in common at least. She didn't say it, but I knew.

No more hiding.

Chapter 6

I couldn't sleep. My entire existence had been completely ripped up and stuck back together, making a whole new life that I could never have even imagined in my wildest, weirdest dreams. The week before, all I ever knew was my little house in the forest with just me and my mother, and the occasional sick or wounded looking for our help. Now I was about to take on the most powerful family in the known world in the most corrupt city on the map.

Funny how things change.

I laid in the dark, completely unhindered from seeing my surroundings. After trying to count sheep and staring hard at the unfriendly and shapeless shadows on the wall, I threw back the quilt and slipped out of my room in search of the kitchen.

Anytime is a good time for food.

By the time I got to the bottom step, I had mastered the art of tiptoeing and continued my little quest for a snack in almost complete silence. There was no one in the dining area or at the bar at this hour. It must've been around three in the morning and the tavern wouldn't be awake for another few hours. Still, I did my best to move silently to the door behind the bar. I let out a small yelp when I tripped over a crouching someone who had apparently been hiding behind the bar the whole time. So much for my secret snack mission. I regained my balance and the croucher had scrambled to their feet to face me.

"Aengel?"

"Saints *alive*, aren't you supposed to be able to see in the dark? "

I was glad she couldn't, because I then realized I was only in my pants and socks. I saw her glare at me through the darkness.

"What are you doing down here?" She squinted in the dark, trying to find my face.

"I was just getting something to eat. What are *you* doing down here? Don't you have a bedroom to be in right now? You know? So you don't have to hide in inconvenient places and trip hungry people on their way to the kitchen."

"It's a secret," she shoved back her wild hair.

"I'm just here for the food," I pushed past her towards the kitchen and hoped she wouldn't follow me and notice the lack of what I was wearing.

But why would I be so lucky?

Not only did she follow me, but she also lit the lantern to light up the whole kitchen with bright yellow light.

"Good *lord*, Eli!" She threw her hands over her eyes and spun away. Laugh or cry, Eli, laugh or cry,

"I told you, I'm just here for the food." I snagged a roll from a basket and then some cheese from the pantry. "How was I supposed to know anyone'd be down here, you can't expect me to dress up every time I walk out my door."

"No," she said with her back still turned. "I just expect you to dress."

"My bad."

"You're bad indeed." She laughed, breaking her angry act.

I shrugged, smiling despite the awkwardness. I had what I came for now, so I started to head back to my room. When I went passed the modest redhead, I noticed she had a kitchen knife on her belt. Not a butter knife. It was the kind you chop heavy-duty meat with. Part of me wanted to ignore it, head back to my room and appease the hunger, the other was too curious for that. I mean, she was hiding behind the bar with a butcher knife, I was interested why.

"What's with the knife?"

She still had her back to me. "Go away, Eli. You're half naked."

"I'm not going anywhere until you tell me."

Unmoved, she said "then you'll be standing there all day, because there's nothing to tell."

"Do you really want to give Sal a heart attack when he comes in here to make breakfast? I mean, I'm sure he's seen a lot in his time, but the sight a shirtless half orc will probably kill him."

She let out a muffled giggle. I smiled. Folding my arms and planting my feet in front of the door, I repeated the ultimatum.

"Everything is fine."

"Clearly. I carry around butcher knives too, just for kicks. I also hide behind bars in the middle of the night. It's comfy, you know?"

"Ooh, me too. Isn't that weird?" She kept her back to me. "Actually," she said. "I might actually need you. I mean, this is what I kept you around for, but it's hard to explain, well, I-"

She paused and went pale, then almost tripped over herself to snuff out the light.

What the-

The door sighed a soft creak as it eased open. I almost slammed my chin on the counter when she pulled me behind Sal's chopping station. She was surprisingly strong for such a small person. In the dark, I could see her trying to make herself invisible against the counter. Trusting in my night vision, I peered over the counter to see one of the men from earlier that day- Wace, Carvel's right hand and esteemed sword wielder. The scar around my leg itched. He skulked into the kitchen and scanned the room for movement. He was human, so my advantage was my vision. His advantage was that he could probably kill me any day of the week, if he found me. Making sure Aengel was still hidden, I prayed he wasn't armed. If I was just a half orc, I'd be useless at sneaking. Seeing how I'm also half elf, I could manage moving silently if I really put effort into it.

He brushed by our hiding spot, and once his back was to us, I slipped out behind him, sliding the cutting board into my hand as I did it.

"Boo."

With all my strength, I cracked the wood over his head, breaking it in two and leaving Wace crumpled on the floor. Dark blood shined on his slicked back hair.

"Eli!" Aengel scrambled over to his limp body and made sure he was still alive.

"What? He deserved it."

She kneeled over him. "Yeah, I guess he did."

"What was he doing here anyways? And why is he looking for you?"

She grabbed a strand of hair, and said something like, "you ask too many questions."

"Fine, I won't pry, but you can't stop me from being concerned." I looked down on the body.

I am a monster.

It was too late now to feel sorry about it. It wasn't every day I crack someone's head open. I prayed he wasn't dead.

She watched with a conflicted look spread across her face as I dragged his body onto the street and left him in some alley four blocks from the Blue Bear. Alone in the dark, lifeless streets, I could smell the blood oozing from his brain, sliding out of his cracked skull. I retched in the street, the smell choking out the contents of my stomach. After a minute or two of puking beside the body, I forced my hands to stop shaking and dragged him farther into the slums. I left him under a pile of stinking garbage, but I could still smell the blood.

The back of the tavern didn't look the same in this light. Neither did the kitchen.

"He was a business partner," she said quietly.

I looked at her. "What kind of business?"

"Czara's the apothecary, I do the numbers, and Wace and the Antimarx take it from there and sell it. Czara and I-"

She swallowed, eyes glued to the floor.

"Czara and I thought we'd try and make a little extra money," she looked up at me. "I didn't want to, but she said it'd be fine, they'd never notice. We gave them sugar, saying it was this new compound she'd been working on. They paid us before they realized what it was."

"Well," I said. "That would explain some things."

She nodded, clearly finished with explaining herself.

The air got too hot in the kitchen, and I excused myself back to my room, leaving the bread roll on the counter. Shatterpoole is *the* drug city. I shouldn't have been so surprised Aengel was involved. I mean, it makes sense for Czara, she looked the part. Aengel though, she still looked like a girl with big green eyes and a glow of innocence.

For the sake of secrecy and safety, when my mother came down from her room, she walked right past me as I was sweeping the dining room before breakfast like she didn't even know me. It stung a little, but I'd rather have my feelings hurt than be dead. The day passed without too much difficulty, but it's not the days that you have to worry about in Shatterpoole.

The sun was setting when I was in the work shed behind the tavern. It had become my little hide-away from the chaos of inside, and I felt like I could really think there. I knew my mother would have thought of a plan of action all day, and then she'd present it to me sometime tonight. We had to do something about the Antimarx before they did something to us, or before they realized why their henchman was missing today. All I had in mind for the Antimarx was that I would do whatever necessary to protect my mother and myself. And Aengel. Whether she liked it or not, she and Sal were my only friends. I would protect Sal, but something told me that he wasn't in too much trouble with any drug lords or powerful warlock families.

Content to just carve a little block of scrap and sit in the straw and wood shavings, the sound of the cutting board cracking his skull dulled to a low whisper in the back of my mind. The smell of the wood almost masked the blood. The hot, metallic blood reeking in my nose. I must've been too absorbed in my work to hear the knocking.

"Eli?" she called, not seeing me yet. "Oh, there you are. What are you doing on the floor?"

"Oh," I pulled myself off the ground. "Hi." She tried to give me a smile, but the confession from this morning was still between us, and I still had blood on my hands.

"We're having a meeting in the kitchen in 10 minutes, don't be late." She nodded and then disappeared into the gray evening.

"I hope it's about my raise," I called after her. Not that I really thought it was about anything like that, I just wanted to pretend for a second the world wasn't a grimy, slimy, dirty place, and make her smile.

I had no way to tell time, so I gauged the passing minutes in the growing shadows. I thought I had done a pretty accurate job until I walked into the kitchen, seeing everyone already assembled. I recognized the strong perfume smell from the night I met Czara as I got closer to the kitchen. There were five people standing around the counter, and I only knew 3 of them. There was Aengel and Czara whispering sharply to each other, and then there was my mother talking to two other women. One was a human who looked about mid-30, but in ranger clothes, a thick, black cloak draped around her shoulders, and a quiver strapped around her. The other was an elf who looked in her 20's, if she was human, with jet black hair that fell to her mid-back and sharp, ice-colored eyes. She looked an awful lot like my mother. They all stopped their conversations when they saw me. I felt the crushing weight of their stares.

The elf my mother was talking to was the first to speak

"So this is your son?" she said. "He looks just like Krill." The human woman came over to me and shook my hand warmly.

"I'm Heartana, you probably don't remember me, you were just a little thing then."

"My name is Rhone, I'm a cousin of your mother." the elf said. She didn't offer a handshake. I noticed Czara glaring at her. My mother cleared her throat.

"Heartana and Rhone were on the elite team that your father and I were also on. I decided to assemble all those who remain of us to help end this hunting once and for all."

"Very inspirational, Lia" Rhone said. "But now that we know our goal, shall we cut the chatting and get down to business? We have an Antimarx to kill here, and Wace." She spat their names like poison.

"What are Aengel and Czara doing here?" I asked. "They probably weren't even alive when Carvel was killed."

"Actually," Rhone began, "Czara was. What are you now? About 30?"

"You wouldn't know."

Rhone ignored her.

"30?" I marveled. Czara looked 17, maybe 18.

"I'm half elf, half-wit." She shot at me with a cruel smirk. She looked me up and down, noting the wood shavings stuck to me and gave a snicker.

That sent the group into an uproar. Me ready to rip that little brat's smirk off her pretty little porcelain face, Aengel holding me back, and the adults trying to help keep us from killing each other.

Chaos, in a word.

Finally my mother and Rhone had me pinned away from Heartana and Aengel holding back the brat.

"Everybody calm down," the older human-woman said. "We aren't avenging anyone if we kill each other in the process."

"Heartana's right." Rhone said. "We kill the more affluent problems, then we can tear each other's throats out. Or try." She added with a smirk directed toward Czara.

"Don't look at me." Czara spat. "I'm betting on you getting caught in the casualties."

Well, this is awkward. I might not have to kill her after all.

"I cause the casualties, little girl." Rhone responded smoothly.

"Tramp." Czara glared with so much hatred, everyone backed up a little.

"Well," Mother cleared her throat, "You two should continue this conversation another time, but now let's get down to business, shall we? There is, as Rhone said, time for these things after we get rid of the Antimarx problem."

"Proceed, cousin." Rhone turned for a final blow at Czara. "I would order you to bed without supper, but your worthy profession does that for me."

"Wait," I said, throwing my hands up. "Am I missing something here?"

"Mistress of the Docks, here, is an unfortunate offspring of my careless youth." Rhone said with a signature smirk, once again, directed at the seething Czara. Aengel looked from one elf to the other, comparing their features just like I was, wonder how we missed the resemblance before.

46

"Oh." I said, initiating a deafeningly awkward silence. I wondered if they were both jerks. Signs pointed to yes.

"Well," my mother continued. "Shall we start our planning then?"

"Sounds good," Aengel said, ignoring the glaring contest between Czara and her mother.

It took well into the night, but we finally all agreed on a plan. All the while, I tried to form the words to tell them Wace was already dead. Every time a chance came up, or it seemed like the right moment, my tongue went numb and my stomach flipped Sal and the other barmaid had to serve dinner around us, careful not to get in the way of our rather dysfunctional scheming. Here's our final product:

Goal: Eliminate Veit and Colonel Steinn Antimarx, the head of the Antimarx family and most enthusiastic towards destroying those who killed his favorite son.

When: The Masquerade tomorrow night at the Antimarx Manor at the center of the city.

How: Poison

Chapter 7

I was elected to be one of the people to actually go inside the manor because I, first off, was the only male in the group, and it was unlikely Veit, or anyone, especially Steinn, would recognize me because Viet had only seen me once and the later never at all. Since it was a masquerade for All Hallows Eve, I would go as myself, secretly hoping to win best costume. I was to escort Aengel, who would be going as, you guessed it, an angel. I guess that made me a devil. They picked her because the Antimarx would kill Czara on sight, but Steinn had never seen her before, and neither had Viet. It was Wace who actually came to *La Tortue Poral* and did the actual dealing, and he was dead. Czara, however, had been to the Antimarx palace, and the other people in the group were already being hunted by them. That left just Aengel and me in the clear.

Once inside, we were supposed find Viet and Steinn, and get Aengel to dance with them, or one of us get close enough to stab them with the poison rings Czara provided.

Of course she had poison rings. She's Czara.

The hardest part won't be getting in, although I expected that not to be a cakewalk, but to get close enough to inject the poison, and get out before we were discovered. I was actually pretty excited for it all, despite it being an assassination and everything. I got dressed up in my only nice clothes, and Aengel found a simple black mask with an old red bed sheet I could wear for a cloak to complete my look. I made sure I also had my father's leather bracelet on to complete the costume, even if it might've caused issues with the mission, seeing that the Antimarx were the only ones who could possibly recognize it and therefore me. It was supposedly lucky, and I needed all the help I could get tonight. I opened my door around 5 o'clock to see the redhead, standing there in a gorgeous white ball gown with yards of glittered tulle and a diamond studded bodice. Magnificent ivory wings spread out behind her, making her look like she had just fallen down from Heaven and landed there in front of me. It was probably stolen, but that really didn't matter at that point.

She smiled.

"We'll be late," she said.

"You look-"

"This is a mission. Get your head out of lala land," she gave me a hard look but I saw her blushing.

"Fine, fine," I shrugged. "Don't take a compliment." I offered my arm, and we glided over the stairs like a real couple about to go to a mask ball, like we were going to actually enjoy the party and not kill two people. My hands just keep getting redder.

"Look at you two," Czara exclaimed when we reached the bottom of the stairs.

"My Rabbit," my mother reached up and cupped my face with her hands. "You look so handsome." That landed me a kiss on the cheek. Mothers. To everyone else in the tavern, this must've looked like *quite* the scene. It's not every day you see an elf kissing an orc-blooded creature. Especially if he's in a devil costume. Everyone in the dining room eyed Aengel like she and her dress had actually fallen from a crack between Heaven and Earth.

The four girls oogled over Aengel for a while before Rhone reeled everyone in and reminded us that we had some drug lords to burn. Sal came out to see us off before Aengel and I climbed into the carriage that Czara somehow had obtained. He was probably more excited for us than anyone else in the whole lower ring, but he had no idea what was actually going on. I honestly thought he was going to cry when he saw Aengel practically glowing in that dress. It took longer than expected, but finally we drove off to the ball.

I wasn't really sure what to say on the ride over there, so I just sat back enjoyed my first carriage ride. It was a lot rougher than I expected, especially while we were still in the outer rings. As we moved into the inner rings, the street were less like Swiss cheese and more like actual streets, making the carriage ride was a lot more smooth. Aengel couldn't stop fixing her hair, even though it was pulled back in a half up-do. The fifth time within five minutes that she reached up to push back these imaginary rebel strands of hair, I grabbed her hand mid-air as gently as a half orc can.

"It's gonna be fine," I vowed.

She nodded, trusting her gaze into mine.

I never let go of her hand.

We pulled up to the massive Iron Gate and watched in awe as it opened to let us onto the cobblestone driveway. The hired footman played his part well by letting us out of the carriage at the grand entrance of the palace as if we were actually nobility. I did my best not to gape at the extreme opulence of the Antimarx palace. Aengel kept me on track, taking my attention away from the house. She stuck out her arm for me to grab, and I managed to get us up the stairs without too much trouble. The colossal red doors were spread open with two bouncers standing on either side of the large entrance, scanning the crowd of incoming party-goers for any unwanted guests. Aengel and I made it past them with her receiving a wink from the particularly blonde bouncer on the left. I ignored it, not wanting to bring attention to ourselves even though I had an extreme urge to do was cave his face in.

There simply aren't enough words in this language to describe the ballroom. Magnificent doesn't even begin to cut it. The white marble room was filled with the spectacularly dressed members of Shatterpoole's aristocracy. Beautiful music filled the vast hall and the dance floor was already filled with high society masqueraders making complex floor patterns that they had grown up learning from private tutors. I needed to avoid dancing if at all possible, I decided. I spotted the food table on the far side of the room.

I got this one.

Aengel grabbed me before I could get too far. "We have a job to do," she whispered. I shot her a look. We searched for the two Antimarx men together at first, but then decided to split up once we realized how many people were at this party. The trick here was to weave through the crowd without drawing too much attention to ourselves, which we both apparently stunk at for our own reasons. I was a giant compared to most of these people, and Aengel was wearing a giant white ball gown and wings. I noticed a man in a black plague doctor mask with those long beak noses that make them look like vultures. He seemed to looking me with an amused half-smile. He strode over to me, and in a smooth low voice as cold as ice he said, "Nice choice of costume," before disappearing into the throng of masked dancers. Before I could go after him, I heard someone say my name behind me.

Aengel looked up at me, studying the confusion on my face. "See someone you know?" she said.

"No, just some guy saying he liked my costume." We both shrugged.

"Follow my lead," Aengel said as she pulled me into position.

"What are you doing?" Touching was off limits for her, I thought.

"*We* are dancing. You've got to know this one, it's the simplest waltz in the known world." She guided me along and spoke the steps out loud in time with the enthusiastic violinists. I stumbled and cursed under my breath, earning us a few stares. She, however, moved effortlessly to the tempo.

"Apparently not simple enough," I said.

"You'll get it."

And I did eventually. After that first song, I did the steps without even thinking about them or mouthing instructions to my feet. We glided across the marble floor through the sea of fellow masked dancers towards the stairway. I could've sworn she was glowing.

Feeling a light tap on my shoulder, I turned from Aengel to find a girl with black hair piled high on her head and dressed in an elaborate crimson ball gown. Her mask suggested that she was also dressed as a devil, and I hoped that because of that she didn't feel some sort of obligation to talk to me.

Grinning broadly, she gave a deep curtsey.

"Mind if I have a turn?"

Aengel hesitated, and released my hand. "Sure."

My new partner danced closer to me than I thought necessary and she smelled strongly of liquor. Fine wine or not, it'll still get you drunk.

"My name's Romania," I could feel her hot breath on me and did my best not to shudder.

"Eli."

She gave a broad smile and stumbled off beat.

I tried to focus on the steps and not my partner, who was clearly in no state to stand, let alone dance.

"My big brother is looking for an Eli you know."

"Your brother?" I kept the edge out of my voice.

"His name is Veit."

Wait, what?

"Where is he? I'd love to meet him."

"Oooh, no, no," she giggled. "Veit doesn't like parties much." She gave me a grave look. "He doesn't really like much of anything."

I twirled her dangerously and she fell into my arms laughing. I pulled her up and tried to scan the room to find any sign of Aengel.

Nowhere to be seen.

I looked deep into Romania's dark, glassy eyes. This was my chance to find him, maybe my only chance before he found me. "Please, it would mean so much to me to meet him." As a half orc, I never thought I'd try flirting as a persuasion tactic, but I guess anything goes on All Hallows Eve in Shatterpoole.

"I couldn't," she squealed. I inched away as discretely as possible.

"Please," I said, cringing inwardly at the whole situation.

"Oh fine," she said. "But he won't be happy."

She took me by the hand and tugged me away from the party and up the grand staircase. We passed several rooms as we entered farther into the manor. The music died away and the only sounds that were left was Romania's mindless talking about the house's history and my own nervous breathing.

An angry cry came from the room at the end of the hall. The open window before the door let in a cold gust of wind from the autumn night. Leaving my latest dance partner behind, I sprinted towards the door and practically ripped it off its hinges.

And found Aengel.

Chapter 8

She was suspended 2 feet in the air, and it might of actually looked like her costume wings were really working if there wasn't an angry 40-something year old man holding her up by her throat. Her face was more crimson than her hair. I wasted no more time observing the scene and launched myself at them. I grappled the man, sending all three of us to the ground. Aengel rolled away as he and I wrestled mercilessly. The guy was strong despite the gray speckling his dark hair. Finally I had him pinned when his hands burst into blue flame, searing my wrists.

Oh right, Warlock family. Fabulous.

With a roar I twisted away from him, clawing at my burns as if that would stop the pain. Aengel was already engaged with him by the time I regained my feet. That girl made up in speed for what she lacked in strength. However, she was at a great disadvantage wearing an enormous ball gown. I pulled her out of the way of a fireball and pushed her toward the door, away from the angry warlock. An arrow came over my shoulder, planting itself in his chest. My mother sprinted past me and was on him in an instant.

What is she doing here? This wasn't the plan!

His fist connected with my mother's skull, making a sickening sound of cracking bone. I jumped on him, sending us both to the ground again. I had him pinned, using my free arm to cave his face in. Blood exploded from his broken nose, splattering my face.

I could smell it.

I stopped and backed away, unpinning the old man.

"RABBIT!"

Then I was on the ground. Above me was my mother engulfed in the blue flame that was meant for me.

The world went silent.

I didn't hear the screams, I didn't hear the crackle of the fire consuming her. I only saw Ma. Dying.

Then she was gone.

Left in her place on the floor where her ashes fell, was a pattern burned in the carpet. It's funny the things that we remember. It almost looked like a rose. Every civil manner I was taught evaporated, and my hesitations were forgotten. I went *wild*. Bloodthirsty and insane with horror and guilt, I tore at him like an animal.

But I wasn't strong enough. None of us were. He was a centuries old warlock who had the power of the ages on his side. Who was I? I was some mongrel from the forest who never had a friend my age before this week.

When darkness washed over me, I prayed it was death.

✦✦✦✦

When I opened my eyes, it was so dark, I was certain it couldn't be heaven. Besides, heaven wouldn't smell damp and rancid. For a moment I was seized with the fear that maybe this wasn't heaven, but could it be...

"Oy! Cell buddy"

Nope. Not dead.

I released a groan into the darkness. Not that it was really darkness to me anyways.

"Aha, so you are alive, aren't ya?"

"Unfortunately," I groaned.

"Come, come. That's no way to be."

"Am I really not dead?" It was still a possibility,

I heard him laugh. He looked young, maybe a little older than me, "No, better than that. You're in the dungeon."

"Oh."

"Hey, don't sound so glum, you're still alive and there is no prison cell that can contain determination."

Wow, really inspiring. I feel sooo much hope right now.

"You're kinda a downer, huh?"

"Kinda." *Does he realize where he is right now?*

"Hey, that's the first positive thing you've said." This joker was getting on my nerves. I was many things in that moment, but positive was not one of them.

"What's your name?" My cellmate said.

"Eli."

"Really? I thought it was Rabbit. That's what the guards said when they threw you in here anyways. They said something about that's what this elf called you. Another assassination attempt on the old man gone wrong. Don't worry, you're not the first to try killing that... You're too young for the words I'd use to describe that man."

I gave a sad chuckle in spite of myself. At least I knew I wasn't the first to fail in killing an Antimarx.

"So which is it," he said. "Eli or Rabbit?"

"Rabbit was my baby name, I'm half orc. I go by Eli these days."

"Ohh, I see. So the elf must've known you for a while."

It felt like I had swallowed a rock. My eyes stung. Burying my face in my hands, I fought to keep the tears in.

"She was my mother."

"Laddie, I'm sorry."

It took me a while, but I eventually pulled myself together. I wiped my face dry with the sleeve of my tunic, stained with blood and ash.

"Was anyone else put in here? Did you see a girl? She's got crazy red hair, she's in an angel costume-"

"Calm down," he put his hands up. "You were the only one brought down here far as I know."

"Thanks," I stood up and found the bars. I tugged on them to test their strength only to find that they were sound. As *extremely* tacky as it might have been, ace over there was right about bars not containing determination. I asked him if he knew how to pick a lock, and we began to compile a list of our available assets to see what we could do about escape. I must've asked him his name at least twice, but he avoided answering every time, so I stopped asking. We spent the next several hours coming up with escape plans that we'd get really excited about it at first, like finally we had *some* hope, but then one of us would point out a major flaw and the idea was regretfully scrapped.

I was sleeping when they came for me. Curled up in as small a ball as I could make myself, I was kicked awake by an unfriendly boot.

"Up orc, the master wants you."

Half orc. Ignoring that little voice in my head screaming at me to stand up and fight, I obediently rose to my feet with as much dignity as I had left, and allowed the four guards to escort me through the dark tunnels to another room below the rays of the sun. It was relatively large compared to my cell, just as bare though. The thought of escaping did cross my mind. That fact that there were four guards escorting me, though, suggested that the same thing occurred to my captors. The room they took me to was all stone, except for the lone figure dominating the center with a cruel smile stitched on his lips.

The beating of my petrified heart drowned out all the other sounds in the dungeon. Breathing was impossible. The room suddenly felt like it was a thousand degrees.

I swallowed.

"What do you want?"

"A man who gets to the point. I admire that." He glided towards me with hands clasped behind his back and spine as straight as a razor blade.

Steinn Antimarx.

I folded my arms to keep them from shaking. "Why didn't you kill me? I'm of no use to you."

"I think, my son," he said reaching up to put his hand on my shoulder, "you are of very much use to me." I jerked away from him and glared.

"I'm not your son."

"Well that's true isn't it? You're technically no one's son now."

All I wanted to do was rip the smirk of his face with my bare hands.

"What do you *want?*"

"You, half-blood. I want you." I was confused to say the least, and was more interested in getting away from him than any information he might give me. It didn't seem like I'd have much of a choice between the two, given my situation. He began to circle me like a hawk circles a rabbit. I stood my ground.

"You'll have to elaborate, I can be a bit of an orc sometimes." I growled.

"But you're also an elf, and that's what makes you so *special.*"

"So I've been told."

"It's so precious how you have no idea." He gave me a solemn smile. "It is true, you are Krill and Lia's son?"

"You oughta know, you killed them." I would've given anything to return the favor.

He straightened himself out and dismissed me, saying that he had enough for today. The guards led me out into the stone hallway and back to my cell. I sat in the darkness, ignoring my cellmate's questions about my absence. I had a lot of things to think about.

Chapter 9

Who knows how long it was before Steinn would call on me again. In those hours of constant nighttime I would lie awake, my head pounding with thoughts. The way the fire swallowed her up, diminishing her to dust, played over and over again in my mind. When I wasn't wondering what would happen if my mother had never found me at all, if I hadn't run away, I prayed that Aengel made it out alive. I drifted in and out of nightmares, my cell mate's mindless chatter keeping me awake for as long as it could. It wasn't enough. The nightmares always came.

It's cold in the forest. Autumn is just beginning to make itself known to the summer drunken inhabitants of the woods. The Tribe is getting ready for the inevitable winter that would blanket our world in a covering of glittering snow in just a few months. Humming while I work, I'm gathering firewood for ma, straying closer to the circle of huts that she and I had been careful to avoid for as long as I could remember.

Then I see them.

Japheth, Ophir, and Ashur.

Supposedly they are the same age as me, but they seem much older since I can hardly look into their grotesque faces without standing on my tip-toes. Even then, I only reach their scarred chins.

Japheth grins to reveal a broken set of teeth that looked like they belonged to a wolf and not a humanoid. But Japheth isn't human, the only blood that runs through his thick veins is the dark, hot blood of an orc.

"Ophir, get me my club, I found a rabbit."

"He looks scared... Aww poor baby." Ashur lets out a low chuckle. They all grip their clubs. They advance.

I run.

Too many times I had stood my ground, only to earn the scars that decorate my body.

I'm fast but not fast enough.

I struggle but it's no use. They grapple me and pin me to the leaf-strewn ground. As Ashur sits on my back, keeping me from escape, I watch Japheth pick up something from the bushes. It's a baby rabbit, no more than a week old, squirming in his rough grip.

He lays it on the ground before me. Then stomps on it. I struggle even harder.

"You have something of mine," Japheth says, his rancid breath blasting in my face.

"No," I managed to gasp under Ashur's impressive weight. "I can't give it to you, ask for anything else, just not-"

"Give it, or you lose a finger."

"What?"

"You heard me, elf."

Ophir grabs my left hand.

"Off you go," he raises it to his cracked lips.

I tear my fist away from his jagged, yellow teeth and slam it in his jutting jaw. Who knows what came over me. Adrenaline shot through my terrified body and I fought like a wild animal. Then next thing I know I'm running like the coward I am. This was a long time in the making, I just needed to find the breaking point. I guess I did.

Running.

Running.

I woke up to the sound of my own screaming as my cellmate shook me awake.

"You alright, laddie?"

Nodding, lying, I said nothing.

I turned over on my side, wishing away this awful place and guilt of not killing Steinn when I had the chance, and then sleep took captive of my mind, again, just like the Antimarxs had taken captive everything else.

I can't feel my legs, I can't move, I can't breathe. I'm suffocating on the darkness. I see nothing.
I see nothing.
"Elliiii"
A voice.
Slow.
Smooth.
Cold.
"Ellliiii" It breathes in my ears.
I try to cry out but only silence escapes my throat.
"Elliii, there's no running now, no more hiding." Terror squeezes my lungs. All I can feel on is the fear.
A coldness creeps over my consciousness. My mind panics like a wasp nest being stomped apart.
Then I see him.

This time, I was pulled out of sleep by that feeling you get when you just *know* someone's watching you, but at the same time you feel completely alone. I wanted to keep my eyes closed because I was safe in my ignorance, for the moment. I opened them though, knowing I had to face the reality sooner or later. It might as well be sooner.

My instinct was right.

"Who are you?" I scrambled to my feet to face the figure standing in the center of my cell looking at me with dark, colorless eyes. His face was impossible to see, hidden behind a plague doctor's mask with the sharp beak pointing at me. Vaguely I recalled him from somewhere, but couldn't place it.

He didn't answer me. He didn't make a sound. The entire air surrounding him seemed to be a vacuum of silence.

My cell mate was nowhere to be seen.

"What do you *want*?"

Silence.

I felt his black stare searing through my panicked thoughts, making me want to run, cry, fight, flee, anything but feel his those eyes on me. Instead of following every instinct of self-preservation screaming at me, I stepped forward.

"Tell me what you want, now."

"I want you, Eli." I knew that voice. Icy enough to send panicked chills down my spine, it was the voice of the man from the ball who commented on my costume. It was the voice from my nightmares.

This should be interesting.

"What about me? Look, I'm really *not* that interesting! I have *nothing* for you! If you want information about my *great adventuring* parents, you're outta luck because they told me almost *nothing* about themselves, and, oh yeah, they're *dead*. And if-"

He gave a low chuckle. "Don't make yourself look a fool, boy. You know too little about yourself to say you have nothing for me."

"I know me better than you ever will," I jabbed a finger at him. "So don't make the mistake of thinking you know me."

"Lost, abandoned, no march to sing,
No master to serve
No death to bring.

Son of the Foul
Son of the Fair
Fill their throne
Be the heir.

Only soul to free them
Only soul to find them
Only soul to summon them
And end this world we see."

I stared at him for a long time after that. My head swam with the words the man in the mask had spoken. So again, I repeated:

"Who are you?"

We stood there for a second that lasted a millennia.

"Missi Mortis." The Prince of Death.

Chapter 10

I'm no theologian, but I knew my basics. In Hell, which is not my favorite topic but we have to go there, there is the Devil, his Prince of Demons, and then the Prince of Death. None of which are particularly pleasant to meet and even less pleasant to have showing up in front of you.

The little I knew about him wasn't comforting.

After revealing his identity, he gave me a choice: I join him to do whatever it is that he wants me for, or he lets the Antimarx kill me. He vanished into the darkness after that, leaving me completely alone in my cell.

I traced mindless lines on the stone floor of my cell with downcast eyes.

He forgot my third choice:

I break out of here.

He left me alone to reflect on my "poor choice", and that's when I forced myself to think of *something*. I couldn't just sit there and wait for them to kill me. Even if my mother was dead, there were still people out there I cared about. I didn't have much time, I was sure about that. I had been here longer than I expected in the first place. There were two guards who ever came near my cell. One was well built and took his job seriously. The other was also enthusiastic about his position as an Antimarx employee, but was not born to be a guard. In fact, I probably could've snapped him in half if I'd really tried, but I'm not about that.

"Dinner" time rolled around, which usually consisted of an old bread crust that's more mold than bread, and some brown water. The guard would slide the tin plate and cut through the 3 inches of space between the bars and the floor, and when I'd finish my "meal", I'd do the same.

The thing is, they have to get close enough to the bars to slide it under.

Skinny was on duty that night.

Maybe it was luck that it was just the small guard, and fate that the more well-suited guard was nowhere to be seen. Either way, the stars had aligned and I took the chance.

Skinny didn't whistle while he worked. His brow was furrowed and he was chewing nervously on his lip when he approached my cell. I think I frightened him. He never once looked me in the eye since I'd been here, which, I'm assuming, was four days. I took the center of my cell and watched him step towards my bars. His eyes flicked up at me for half a second before he bent down to slid the food through.

It was now or never.

The second he bent down, I sprang to the bars and grabbed at his feathery hair. He cried out in surprise and then pain as I slammed his face against the metal bars over and over until he went limp.

"Sorry."

He was unconscious, not dead, thank heavens. I was done with killing people, if I could help it. Unsure of how much time I had before someone came or he'd wake up, I dragged him into the position where I could grab his keys and unlock the door. I worked quickly, but my shaking hands didn't make it easy. I dropped the keys and the sharp sound of metal hitting stone rang through the dungeon.

I stopped.

After a minute of hearing no sounds of concern for the loud noise coming from the holding cell area, I thanked my luck again and continued trying to free myself. Finally I heard the lock spring open and the door shifted outwards an inch.

I smiled.

The hallway was quiet as far as I knew, no suspicious sounds coming from any direction. It was my perfect moment.

Just try and take me now, I dare you. I almost started humming while I walked down the hall towards the guards' room and the exit.

There was no way they'd get me back in there.

A noise came from around the corner, stopping me in my tracks. Heart pounding and newfound confidence pretty much gone, I flattened myself against the wall and waited for the unlucky pedestrian to cross me.

A minute passed, then two.

Fed up with waiting, I gave into my impatience and spun around the corner.

I slammed into her.

"Arh! Get *off* me!" A little fist crashed into my stomach. I'm built like a bear and she's built like a china doll, so the intended damage was not delivered, despite her effort.

"Aengel!" Even if she had just given me a bruise, I was beyond happy to see her. She stopped and looked up at me in the darkness. I knew her human eyes wouldn't be able to recognize me in the dark.

"Eli?"

"Yeah," I refrained from hugging her. Just knowing she was alive was enough.

"What are you doing out here?"

"Um, escaping. What are *you* doing?"

"Rescuing you."

"Oh." I shrugged. "Well, here I am."

"I can see that," she smiled. "Czara is back down the hall with one of the guards, we should probably go get her then."

"Is she okay?"

"Czara? Oh, she's fine." Aengel waved her hand. "She can hold her own."

We snuck back down the hallway, careful not to raise suspicion that anything out of the ordinary was happening in the dungeon. The further we got down the hallway, the louder the muffled noises got. Finally I identified the sounds as someone screaming with a gag shoved down their throat. The half elf was sitting on the tied up other guard.

"Oh good, you're alive," she said, briefly looking up at me.

"Nice to see you too, Czara."

"We should keep moving," Aengel warned. "They'll figure out something's up any minute now." Both of us half elves agreed with her. We stole out of the guard's service entrance and into the autumn night. Inhaling the fresh air and drinking in the starlight, I remembered how much I'd missed the outside world. Not that I really forgot I was missing it while I was sitting in a rancid-smelling basement for the past few days, but I certainly had a new appreciation for it.

Once we were on the street behind the Antimarx manor, we changed our gait to a nonchalant stroll, as not to draw attention to ourselves. Walking down the cobblestoned street by all the large houses owned by the most powerful in the city, I wondered what it might be like to live in one.

"Sorry we took so long getting you," Aengel said, derailing my train of thought. "There was some turmoil when I told the others what happened to your mother." I didn't respond because I wasn't really sure what to say. "I'm sorry," she said quietly.

"I'm sorry I didn't kill him when I had the chance."

"It's no one's fault but Steinn's. Don't blame yourself."

I looked at her, begging for someone to understand. She either ignored me or just didn't see.

"Rhone and Heartana left. Rhone is arranging the funeral with the elves, Heartana went with her. You should go."

I shook my head. It would be too painful. The elves would probably throw up in their mouths if they saw me anyways. I was the most disgusting freak of nature of the inconceivable mind to them, and I didn't need any more enemies at the moment.

We walked in silence until Czara ignored the fragile state of the moment. "So Eli," she said turning to me. "I guess we're related."

Well, our mothers were cousins. "Yeah, I guess we are."

Mistaking my response for an invitation to recount our entire family history, she only finished climbing our family tree once we reached the Blue Bear Inn and Tavern. Apparently adventuring ran in the family, and so did textile trading, but that's not really as exciting to think about.

When Sal saw the three of us coming through the kitchen door, he nearly sobbed with joy.

"Aengel!" He threw his skinny arms around her and practically soaked her shoulder with tears of joy.

"I'm okay, Sal." She pulled away from him and looked to Czara, then me. "We're all going to be okay."

"Eli! My boy!" His embrace was more forceful than I expected from a man of his age.

"Sal! You're going to crush him!" Aengel laughed. "Come on, Eli, let's get you upstairs and I'll bring you something once you've clean up."

I smiled, despite the fact I was on the verge of tears, "do I smell *that* bad?" Aengel was about to open her mouth, but Czara beat her to it.

"Yeah, pretty much."

We all laughed except Czara, who still wore the grimness I kept inside. Aengel and her shooed me upstairs to my room where I took the longest bath in working memory and pulled on my old clothes- my new ones were completely ruined after my stay at the Antimarx, free-of-charge inn. I traced my finger over the stitches in the cloth where a sword almost took off my leg. Once changed, I laid on my soft, white bed. Every time I closed my eyes, the darkness never stayed empty. There was always fire, there was always blood, and there was always the pain. This ache in my chest that reminded me that not only have I seen death, but I'd caused it. Someone knocked on my door. I got up, made myself presentable, and then turned the knob.

Aengel pushed her way in, carrying a tray piled with steaming food.

"Let me help you with that," I started to reach for the tray.

She shook her head. "No, no. I got it." She placed it on my desk and then turned to leave.

"Aengel, wait," I said before she made it out the door. I didn't want to be alone just yet, not while I could only thing about the fire scorching her pale skin, not while I could still smell the blood.

"Yeah?"

"Thanks."

She smiled. "Anytime." Pausing, she turned back to me. "You know, I was going to wait until morning to ask, but it's been killing me."

"No, go ahead. You ask, I'll eat." I grabbed the bowl of mashed potatoes with extra butter melted into it. Sal knew me well. Maybe I could get over this pain.

"Why didn't the Antimarx kill you? I mean, you were unconscious in their house, and perfectly vulnerable. Those of us who weren't barely escaped with our lives. I'm just curious why they didn't kill you when they could've. Easily."

"Well I'm glad you think killing me is so easy," I sounded crueler than I meant to, but humor was a little difficult to come by these days.

"I'm serious, Eli. When the Antimarx spare someone, it's usually because they have something better than killing them in mind." She was looking at me with those green eyes, like she knew I had something to say.

"Honestly, I don't really know what they want. Steinn did call a meeting with me once, but all we talked about was that my parents were the Krill and Lia he killed. Then there was this other guy... I'm pretty sure it was all in my head though. Eating rotten food does things to you." I forced a shrug.

"What do you mean?" She said, eyes glowing with curiosity.

"I had this- I don't know- encounter? With um," I paused, not really sure how to say it. "I think I talked to Missi Mortis..."

The eyes widened with horror. "*The* Missi Mortis?"

"Plague doctor mask, creepy voice, soulless eyes. Yeah, I think so."

"You better hope on your soul it was the rotten food." She brushed back a lock of rebellious red hair. "What did he say?"

"You know, I'm not really great on memory, but I think he said that he wanted me for something and then recited this really weird poem about some sort of heir. I don't really know."

She looked at me with a frightened concern.

"We should ask Czara about it," she said at last.

"Why?"

"Because she's an expert on all things Mortis."

"Really?" Leave it to Czara to know all about the Prince of Death.

"Yes, but I'm sure only God knows why."

She slipped out into the hallway to go find our Mortis-expert. I heard her fumble down the stairs to find Czara, who was probably making herself at home by the bar. They returned a couple minutes later with the half elf sporting a slightly annoyed expression, small glass in hand.

"Aengel said you had something interesting to tell me."

Both girls seated themselves on my bed as I paced the room, trying to recount as much of my story as I could. They say the devil is in the details. Once I had sufficiently expressed as much as I could remember, we all looked at Czara for her take on Mortis's interest in me.

"Well," she said at last. "It doesn't look good."

"Oh really? I didn't guess that yet." I snorted.

"Save it, orc. Do you want my help or not?

I heaved a reluctant sigh. Being pushed around by a little half elf girl wasn't my idea of fun on any day of the week.

"*Half* orc," was all I said.

She gave me a victorious smirk and continued. "I know there's a prophecy that talks about an heir. I forget it though, there's a lot of prophecies out there."

"So what do we do now?" Angel twisted a piece of red hair around her fingers, looking from me to Czara, and then to me again.

"We go the Mortis's temple and find a copy of the prophecy." Czara said it like it was obvious. I shifted uncomfortably and crossed my arms in front of my chest. Going to the temple of the Prince of Death sounded like an unpleasant experience, especially if he was interested in me joining him for whatever evil purpose he had in mind.

"Okay," I said. "Let's go tomorrow then."

The half-elf got up to leave. "You'll want to get a good night's sleep." And with that she returned back to the bar.

Chapter 11

The temple turned out to be a small basilica just outside the city. The building looked like it had been abandoned for years and a gloom hovered over it, signaling the nature of its patron. It would've taken too much time to walk, so we borrowed horses from one of Czara's friends and set off early in the morning. Distantly, I wondered how Czara was so well connected, and then remembered she was an apothecary who was in high demand.

Chills shot through my nervous system as we neared the crumbling stone building. I ignored them and urged my burdened horse on, sweat collecting on my palms. The temple was on the top of a steep hill, so we parked our horses at the bottom and made the rest of the journey on foot. Aengel had the most difficulty going up the steep incline because she was the only one in a dress. The only clothes Czara ever wore were tight and black leather, maybe a red bodice sometimes. I, obviously, wore pant and a shirt like most underclassmen.

We finally made it up the hill to the basilica in one piece, although I was a little winded. Climbing giant hills wasn't on my list of normal activities. The entrance was sealed by a massive iron door, taking up most of the space of the front of the building. My large fist sent vibrations through the metal as I pounded on it, hoping someone inside would answer.

The place looked like it hadn't been inhabited for decades. We stood there for a couple minutes in silence while we waited. I fidgeted with my bracelet, rubbing the worn leather between my fingers At last the iron gave way and shifted to reveal a man wearing the complete, dirty-white plague doctor uniform: crow mask that concealed his entire face, and a long, thick robe that fell to the floor with a hood hanging low over his masked eyes. It was definitely a fitting look for the place.

"Can I help you?" The voice was muffled under the fabric.

"Yes, Father," Czara said. It was the first time I saw her show anyone respect besides her own reflection. "We are looking for a copy of a prophecy."

"Come in," after shepherding us inside, he closed the iron door and began down the long stone sanctuary with other priests scattered about inside. "We keep our documents in the Archives, Brother Ornias will show you." He grabbed an unsuspecting priest who was slouching against one of the many crumbling pillars, staring out the dirty window. The first priest dragged him away from us for a moment, scolding him for something thing or another before coming back to us.

"How might I help you?" Even if his voice was muffled, I could tell he was about my age, maybe a year older.

The elder priest cleared his throat. "Take them to the Archives and help them find what they need."

"Certainly," he turned and led us to the back of the sanctuary into one of the halls breaking away from the center of the building. As we walked down the dark corridor, he asked us what exactly it is that we were hoping to find.

I tried to find more descriptive words, believe me, but they escaped me. "We're looking for this prophecy of Missi Mortis that mentions something about an heir and mentions a "them" a lot at the end..."

"It's not like Missi Mortis is one of the oldest and most powerful demons in the spiritual world with thousands of prophecies and legends about him."

The three of us looked at him with blank frustration,

"I thought you were an expert," Czara said.

The young priest turned his head at her for a moment, and then turned it away. "Forgive me if your friend is slightly nondescript."

"Do you have a problem, temple-boy?" I growled.

"Do you want your prophecy?"

"Why else would I visit this lively, colorful place?"

"Eli," Aengel put a hand on my arm as we continued to follow him down the hallway, pulling it back quickly so she didn't have a vision. I heaved a deep breath and finally we reached a large wooden door that looked like it had seen better days.

"Here we are," Brother Ornias opened the door. The Archives was slightly bigger than my bedroom at the Blue Bear, littered with stacks upon piles of stacks of old documents and ancient tomes.

"This could take a while," he breathed. "Can you tell me *anything* else about this prophecy? We could be here for years if all I have to go off of is that 'it's something about an heir and a them'".

"Well," I wasn't sure how much I could trust him. But what choice did I have? "Missi Mortis came to me and said I was needed for some purpose. Then he recited this poem that sounded a lot like a prophecy."

The priest turned to the girls. "Is he serious?"

"Unfortunately," Czara hissed.

"Well," the priest turned back to me. "At least there's only one prophecy with an orc mentioned in it."

"Lucky me."

"Lucky indeed, that prophecy was my priesthood exam. I had to memorize it to pass."

"That is lucky." I knew there was a God up there, but I didn't know He looked out for the likes of me.

"No need to look for it, I'll write it down." Once he located a blank piece of paper and a pen with some ink, he scrawled this in fancy handwriting:

Lost, abandoned, no march to sing,
No master to serve
No death to bring.

Son of the Foul
Son of the Fair
Fill their throne
Be their heir.

Only soul to free them
Only soul to find them
Only soul to summon them
And end this world we see

We all hovered over the priest while his pen scratched at the parchment. When he finished, we stood there in silence, reading and re-reading what he had written.

"So," Aengel said. "Does that mean you can free these people or something?

"Something like that," the priest turned around to face us. "It means he can raise Mortis's demon army."

"Oh," I couldn't breathe for a moment. I couldn't really do anything, actually, except for stare. Everyone looked at me with deep concern- except the priest, I couldn't actually see his face, but he was looking at me too.

"What?" I wished they'd stop looking at me, what was I supposed to do? Suddenly Steinn confirming my parentage made sense, and so did Mortis's confusing statement about how I knew so little about myself. He was right.

"You have a couple options," the brother said. "You can take advantage of the prophecy and raise a demon army that will most likely destroy all that is good and beautiful in this world, you can run and hide and let Mortis find you and make you do this, or you can kill Mortis. Either way, you've got your work cut out for you.

"Do I have any other options?" None of the above sounded particularly appealing at the moment. Honestly, I just wanted to go hide in the forest and will it all away, but that obviously won't work.

"No, actually." He adjusted his mask and stood up. "But, there's a legend-"

Czara breathed a heavy sigh.

The priest ignored her and continued. "The prophecy was written by a very powerful aspicien whom Mortis consulted with often. Mortis had angered the heavens and there was vicious, bloody war between good and evil."

We all leaned in.

"Evil lost, as it usually does, and Mortis's army was taken from him by the angels."

"What happened to them? The army, that is." Aengel brushed back her hair that had fallen over her eyes again.

"They were tucked away somewhere in the cosmos. It's not really a matter of *where* they are, it's a matter of *who* can summon them, and Mortis lost that power. But you can't just have a master less demon army floating around, so the angels gave the power to someone who would likely never exist. Well," he turned to me. "I'm not actually sure why the angels do what they do, evil's motives are much easier to figure out."

Czara snorted.

"Yes, the angels gave you the power to raise an army, but the legend is that what we have here is only half of the prophecy."

I looked up. "Half?"

"The thing about God, good, light, whatever you want to say, is that there's always a choice. You can raise Hell, but it would be uncharacteristic of Heaven to give you only one option- especially if that only option is to do evil."

"Oh." I thought for a moment. "So you think the aspicien only gave Mortis half the prophecy? Why would they hide the truth?"

Czara laughed. "Don't be so naive, Eli, he would've killed her if she gave him bad news."

"How'd you know it was a her?"

"Aspiciens are always girls," Aengel chimed in.

"I'm assuming she *did* tell him the truth," the priest said. "Because the legend also says she was killed once the prophecy was composed. He probably destroyed the part he didn't like and kept the part he did."

"Sounds like Mortis," Czara folded her arms, narrowing her icy eyes at the piece of paper with the prophecy on it. I fought the urge to inch away from her.

"So what now?" I hated the forbidding gloom hovering in the air. It was unsettling. "Do we try and kill him? Do we try and destroy his army? Do we look for the second half of the prophecy?"

Czara looked shocked for once. "You aren't even considering the option of complete dominion over a legion of demons?"

We all looked at her.

"No, Czara. I'm not."

She tossed her hands up. "I'm *just* saying."

"How do we kill Mortis?" Aengel pointed out. "It's not like he's mortal."

Our priest puffed his robed chest out jokingly, "funny you should mention that. I happen to know,"

"Care to enlighten us?" I said, sounding more like Czara than I meant to.

"The pretty girl is right, he's not mortal," Aengel glared at him, despite the fact he was agreeing with her. "But he does have a soul, which can be destroyed."

"How?" I said.

"It's called the Animula, it holds Mortis's soul."

I guess the fancy word lost me. "So, what exactly is it?"

"It's a sword," he said it like it's something I should've known.

"Right-o..." I looked back at the piece of paper with my fate written on it.

Only soul to free them
Only soul to find them
Only soul to summon them
And end this world we see

The words kept ringing over and over in my head. Suddenly the room felt very small. I needed to get out of there. I needed to get somewhere quiet, somewhere alone. Too many people were expecting too many things from me. I was just a weird mix of orc from a little forest tribe that that never did anything out of the ordinary and my only expectation was to survive. Now, I suddenly had a fate that was more than I could handle.

"Give me a second," storming out of the little Archive room, I made sure to close the door behind me. Not really sure of where I was going or what I was going to do when I got there, I practically ran down the stone corridors of the temple.

Out. I need to get out.

My head was spinning. I found an empty alcove in some distant hallway, and slumped down against the wall underneath the dirty, stained glass window. Burying my face in these monster hands, I let the thoughts, fears, memories, horrors, and those *words* rain down on me. There was nothing and everything I could do. Choosing the evil option was out of the question, obviously, but what about those gray areas? The easiest thing was to run and hide. It was very tempting. The next best thing was to find the Animula and kill Mortis. Then there was the most noble, but hardest option: we kill Mortis and find the second half of the prophecy- destroying him and his demons forever.

I almost laughed out loud at how dramatic it all sounded.

Me? The guy they used to call "Rabbit"? Was I really qualified to deal with this kind of stuff? I didn't think so. Someone touched their hand to my arm for a fraction of a second. Looking up, those bright green eyes were staring back at me.

"You look like you could use a friend."

I let out a sound of pure exasperation. "How'd you know?"

"Lucky guess," she slumped down next to me. "So what's the verdict? This is all you, Eli, Czara and I are willing to help out how ever we can."

"No pressure," I muttered to myself.

We sat there for a while, just sitting. I weighed each option in my mind, and tried to decide what was holding me back. On the ground of that stone hallway, I had to decide what was important, what was it that, at the center of my being, that I valued. I stood.

"I've decided."

Aengel struggled to keep up with my eager gait back to the Archives. I threw open the door to find the priest and Czara pouring over old tomes, gather whatever information they could about our opponent.

"Everyone," I announced. "I'm gonna kill some demons, who's with me?"

Chapter 12

Brother Ornias was the first to speak up.

"I'm in."

"Me too."

"Well I'll do it," Czara said. "But not because I owe you any favors." I smiled and ignored her jerk-ish-ness, for the moment.

"Wait," I turned to the priest. "Why are you helping us? Aren't you supposed to worship Mortis?" He was, after all, his priest. I was surprised he even mentioned killing his patron demon.

"I'm sorry, you must have mistaken me for someone who actually wants to be a Priest of Death."

"So you'll help us?"

He snorted. "You're going to need me." We all shot him glares. "I know more about Mortis than the three of you combined."

"Fine, but lose the attitude."

"Will do, Captain."

"Good, now let's get out of here, this place gives me the creeps."

We followed our new team member down the halls and finally out the door. Every time we passed another priest on the way to the door, I wondered if they also would have joined us given the chance. I mean, you have to be a certain kind of person to willingly worship a demon. He walked out with us, not even saying good-bye to any of the other priests or gathering any of his belongings. I thought this was strange, but kept it to myself while we made the journey back down the treacherous hill and through the forest to the Blue Bear. The girls shared a horse, and us guys each had our own; Partly because the girls were pretty light and we didn't want to overcrowd the horses, and partly because I didn't want the girls getting too close to a stranger we knew literally nothing about. Before the high walls of the city were in sight, the priest ordered us to stop. He got off his horse and yanked off the thick white fabric. We all gaped at him in shock of his utter lack of shame and the fact that he turned out to a boy of about 17 years with dark blonde hair and piercing blue eyes, wearing a black leather jacket and tall black soldier boots to match.

"I'm guessing that's not temple uniform," Czara smirked.

He gave her a small smile, "no, no it is not." He sauntered over to the girls' horse and locked eyes with the half elf. "You can call me Luce."

She wasn't impressed, and if she was, she was an amazing actress. "I'll call you whatever I feel like calling you, but I'll consider the suggestion." I just looked at him, hoping we'd all get along long enough to kill Mortis. He ignored her and got back on his horse after tossing his robes into the underbrush.

"You just gonna leave them there?" I looked at the littered robe crumpled on the side of the road.

"I don't need or want them anymore."

"They might be useful later," I said. Besides, my mother always would emphasize respecting the forest. She was drilling that into me from the time I could talk, abandoning that now would be worse than if she was still alive. I slid off my horse and grabbed the robes and threw them at him before mounting again. No one spoke as we rode back towards the city in the fading light.

I got acquainted with my horse while I struggled not to fall off. I didn't know much about horses and never mastered riding them. The little riding experience I did have came from the animals my mother healed for some of the Tribesmen or travelers just passing through. When I was about 11, a knight came through with a beautiful black warhorse with broken leg. It was a pretty nasty break, the kind that came from fighting. The knight stayed nearby in the forest just to make sure he could see her each day, which I thought was pretty nice of him. I never knew much about the knight, but the horse liked me a lot. Most animals do, for some, strange reason. Once she was better, the knight took the chance to teach me to ride. At first, I couldn't stop violently bobbing up and down like a loose water pump. Not only did it make for a rough ride, it left my flank as sore as the horse's. Eventually I learned how to lean back and position myself better so traveling by horseback wouldn't be as exhausting and painful, although still difficult. I never quite got the hang of it, but I do improve each time. Generally I avoid traveling by horseback, not that I ever got much chance to ride the forest. Everything we ever needed was usually within walking distance. The horse was patient with me while returning to Shatterpoole. It had been a while since I'd been on horseback. I thanked her once we arrived back at Czara's friend's stables with a sugar cube and a grateful pat on her furry head.

The stables were located in the same outer ring as the Blue Bear, so it didn't take us long to walk back. As we walked, Luce drew many stares and blushed glances from the young city girls. He hardly noticed, taking in the sights of the city like it was a whole new world. Maybe it was.

Sal saw the four of us coming through the back door and gave us a warm welcome back, typical Sal. He was very interested in our new companion, although the stranger deflected all questions asked of him besides his name. He was intelligent, that much was obvious. He clearly didn't get out much either. Aengel didn't seem to mind him terribly, but she kept her distance. She set him up with a room, and we all met in the dining room to discuss our plans over dinner.

Luce leaned dangerously over his bowl of stew. "Most of the legends claim that the Animula is hidden somewhere in the mountains of the North, but a couple say that it's hidden in Franken."

"Franken?" I had no idea what he was talking about.

His blue eyes glittered with excitedly. "The country across the sea. It's-"

"There's other countries outside of Nyverden?" I only realized how ignorant I sounded the second the words came out. Out of respect for the guy who can summon a demon army, the three of them suppressed their mockery. I could see it almost physically pained Czara to hold back the snarky remark on the tip of her tongue. Luce didn't skip a beat.

"There are a few countries besides Nyverden out there. There's Franken, Worglo, and Taharia. I'll find you a map sometime. The only one you have to worry about for the moment is Franken, because that's where I, personally, suspect the Animula to be."

"Why?"

He smiled. "Brief summary of Franken, because time is short: It's an icy wasteland ruled by very unfriendly dragons who sometimes take the form of kind-of-humans."

Czara raised an eyebrow. "What is that supposed to mean?" Aengel looked up from our conversation and noticed the crowd starting to form around our table. I had been so intrigued with my expanding world, that I hadn't realized curious travelers gathering around to listen to Luce's story. Aengel and I shared a look, knowing that we couldn't discuss our plans with so many ears around to hear it. Luce must've noticed too. He started to go off about the human-like creatures the dragons shapeshift into and some legend on how they got to do that. Not really interested in shapeshifting legends (they always kind of freaked me out), I watched the way the light from the great fireplace caught on Aengel's flaming hair, how the shadows played across people's faces, changing as they engaged in conversation or listened to a great tale of an exaggerated past.

I saw him.

It was like a horse just kicked me in the lungs. The sharp beak of the mask glinted menacingly in the orange firelight. I stood up. Every sound died, fear took over.

"Eli!" Aengel was standing, everyone else looking at me. I looked back to where I'd seen him by the wall but he was gone. I felt sick.

"Uh, sorry." I pushed myself away from the table, escaping to my work shed out back

He looked so real, I couldn't have imagined him.

Frantically, I searched around the shed, inside and out, tearing the place apart for any signs of the man in the black mask was there. Every piece of unfinished furniture was turned over and every shadow searched before I could convince myself I was safe. I stood in the middle of the small shed trying to stop breathing like a maniac, my heart fluttering like a swarm of angry bats.

"Something on your mind?" Aengel slid through the old, wooden door and picked up her chair laying on its side near the workbench. She leaned back on the unfinished chair and studied my face. "You look like Hell."

"Thanks."

"I mean it, you really need to pull it together."

I looked up at her, looking so collected and beautiful on that half made chair. "I thought I saw Mortis just now."

Her eyes widened with surprise. "In the tavern?"

"Yeah."

She looked me up and down. "That's not good."

"No kidding," my voice came out shaky. I studied the straw-covered ground in despair. "We can't fight him right now, there's no way we'd win."

"I was kind of talking about how you're seeing people who aren't there. I mean, that's just concerning." She smiled and reached out to pat my arm before stopping herself mid-air. Aspeicien. "We'll get him soon," she promised.

"You think so?"

"Sure I do."

I sighed, trying to believe her enough to convince myself.

"I don't know if I can do this."

"Eli, enough with the self-doubt. It's getting concerning." She softened her tone. "Now calm down, and tell me, what's our plan?"

I stood up, feigning the confidence I didn't feel. She was right, I needed to stop this. It wasn't helping anyone.

"We leave for Franken."

Chapter 13

The gray dawn sent mist covering the ground, turning the sky the same opaque color. Trying not to fall off my horse, I led her north with my team trailing behind: me, Luce, Aengel, and Czara. The night before, once Luce's audience got tired of him talking about the science of shape shifting dragons, I announced that we would be riding to Franken in the morning. Not that the mountains didn't seem like a possible place for Missi Mortis's Animula, but there were too many rumors of it. Mortis knew how to control gossip, judging by his age and power and everything else, so it'd be more likely for the lies to spread more frequently than the truth he didn't want anyone knowing. The only reason we even had a suspicion it was north was because Luce read it in one of the first priests' accounts before he mysteriously disappeared. I was convinced.

Sal insisted that each of us dig through the collection of stuff inattentive customers left behind to get some backpacks and other traveling equipment. Each of us ended up with a backpack and a bedroll, and two tents for us all to share. Sal made sure we well stocked with food too, being the doting man he is.

"Ya sure ya hafta ta go to, missy?" Two of us looked up because "missy" sounds a lot like "Missi". One of us looked up because that's what her stand-in father called her.

"I'm sure."

Sal looked like he was about to burst.

"I'll be back," she patted his wrinkled hand. "I'll be back before you know it."

The old man looked at the rest of us, nodding as he met each of our eyes.

"You take care of my Aengel, ya hear?"

"We will, Sal. Don't you worry."

He took her hand. "You're just like your mother. She could never stay in one place very long."

She smiled. "You be good while I'm gone."

We started off with heavy packs, riding out of the city and into the same forest I came from. I lead the way with Luce navigating. He studied the maps and geography of Nyverden more than any of us, so we made him in charge of finding our route. I silently prayed we didn't bump into the Tribe.

That would just be awkward.

The green from the leaves had transformed into the fiery colors of autumn. A chill stung the air, pulling clouds of frozen breath from our mouths

"Fearless leader," Luce called out to me over the sound of the horses. "Just thought I'd let you know there's a town ahead." He pulled his horse up next to mine with ease and pointed to a small black dot on his worn map of the Goldleaf Forest. I tried to see if my tribe was on there, but he pulled it away too quickly

Even though it felt like we were riding for hours, we had left early morning and it was only around the afternoon by the time I seriously considered walking for a while.

"Luce, how long until the town did you say?"

"A couple hours." He consulted his map again. "We'll be there before sunset."

Each of the girls had their own horse, and seemed to be faring better than I was. It looked like Aengel had a lot of experience with riding. More than once I saw her bending down and whispering in the animal's brown, furry ear. I wondered if her aspicien powers worked on animals too. I mean, it worked on me after all. Czara took up the rear, her horse trotting nonchalantly behind Aengel's with no interest in passing anyone anytime.

Sore and hungry, I was beyond ready to call for a lunch break when the sun reached well overhead.

"Lunch, guys!"

Everyone let out a sigh of relief when we all slid off our horses.

If I ever get rich, I patted my horse lightly on her brown shoulder, *I'm going to get a carriage and never ride a horse again.*

"Let's see, what do we have for food here." I peeled back the flap of my backpack and found some Sal-made sandwiches waiting for me underneath the fabric.

I was halfway through my second one when I noticed everyone looking at me.

Czara raised an eye brow.

"What?"

"You eat like an animal."

I was about to say something rude when Luce looked up from his map and said, "So what's the plan exactly."

All eyes on me.

"Well, we go to Franken, find the animula, and then kill Mortis."

"That's pretty well formed," he muttered before letting his eyes drift back to the map.

"You do realize the animula is a magical weapon right?" Czara mentioned.

Aengel raised her hand.

"Yes?" I said.

"Don't you need specific training with magical weapons?"

Czara smiled. "Someone did her homework."

"What does that mean for us then?" I said.

"We'll have to find you someone who knows how to use an animula against a greater demon. Otherwise you might end up killing the wrong person, yourself included," Luce hardly looked up from the map.

"Okay…"

Czara patted my arm like I was a lost puppy. "Fear not, orc, I already know just the person."

"That makes me feel so much better." I can only imagine the kind of person she had in mind.

"So let me get this straight," Aengel said. "We go to Franken, somehow manage to find a sword in miles and miles of frozen wasteland, then find this guy who's gonna teach Eli how to use the darn thing before we finally get to kill Mortis?"

I shrugged. I guess this was more of a process than I thought.

We had to pick up our pace by the time the light started to fade so, like all town gates at sunset, the one at the town we were riding to wouldn't close on us. Thankfully luck was shining down on us with the last rays of autumn sun. The large wooden doors were still yawning open when we rode up, inviting us into the little trading post town. I noticed a watchman squinting down at us from his perch on the timber wall and quickly looked away. I didn't have to meet the guy to tell he was unfriendly.

Quiet and tired, there were only a couple of citizens on the dim-lit streets this time of evening. It was strange. This would be about the time of day when the town's nightlife reanimated, but it looked like everyone was closing themselves up in their houses.

Literally.

I noticed a man nailing a scrap of wood over his windows. Everyone looked nervous.

The four of us were studied with awe by the children and suspicion by their parents. I wasn't sure whether to feel relieved or anxious when we reached the town's tavern marked with a fading sign reading: Goldleaf Inn. We put our horses in the marked stables and entered into the strangely quiet dining room. It was smaller than the Blue Bear, but cozy. I thought the tavern was empty when we first walked in, but then noticed the slew townspeople huddled around an animated old man by the simmering fire place.

"And he comes out only when the sun goes down-" the old man's eyes held mine from across the room while he continued the story he was telling when we four walked in. I shivered.

"Can I help you?" A guff, middle-aged man wearing a greasy apron stood in front of us, looking at Luce, hands on hips.

I stepped forward. "We need some rooms and food. Our horses are in the stables, so you can add that on to our bill too." He looked a little surprised, but quickly shook it off for the sake of business. It's not every day you see an orc speak like that to a human, I knew that.

"Certainly," he took out a small brown leather book, to keep records I assumed. "Can I get a name?"

"Eli."

"Eli What?" His beady eyes flicked up at me, jeering, menacing. Orcs don't have last names. This sets them even lower on the racial hierarchy, we're usually considered no better than a horse by most people, especially outside the cities. I thought for a moment, I never really needed a last name before, and never really spent time thinking if I even had one. That just goes to show my limited experience outside the forest.

"Krillson," I said at last. That was the first thing I could come up with. Nothing fancy, just my father's name with "son" mashed on the end, which was the human custom.

Each of my companions avoided sharing glances while the man was serving us, but once he had his back turned to show us our rooms, they all exchanged those surprised looks. *Since when did Eli have a last name? Since when did orcs order humans around?*

Since now people, since now.

We got two rooms, courtesy of Czara and Aengel-
the only ones with money. The priest and I had no cash to
speak of, unfortunately. Aengel still owed me pay for all
those hours I worked for her at the Blue Bear anyways, so I
tried not to feel too bad about it although I planned to pay
her back. The girls got a room, and Luce and I shared the
second. They weren't nearly as nice as the ones back at the
Bear, but they were more comfortable than sleeping
outside. I noticed bars on the windows. Once we all put our
stuff down, we met up in the dining room by the circle of
enthralled listeners and the old man. I listened to him while
I spooned the thin soup into my mouth. The four of us were
still too tired from traveling all day to talk.

"How did it all start?" One of the listeners, a young
boy, looked up at the gray-haired man.

"How? My boy, that is the true mystery. Some say
he was cursed by a jealous enchantress, others say he
begged the form upon himself from the Devil's own hand."
I leaned closer to the group, scooching my chair over just a
little. "All we can know, my friends, is that he comes out at
night and he dances with chaos and destruction."

That's not dramatic at all.

After the old man went on about all the carnage and
terror that "he" wrecked upon the town, I got tired of
guessing who "he" was. I'm not one for patience.

My presence became known immediately when the
old man paused to watch me join their huddle. My friends
watched curiously from our table. Luce had a goofy grin on
his face, laughing at their confused reactions.

An orc? I saw their mouths gape like stupid fish.
*What would he want with us? Who does he think he is
coming over here and-*

"So, who is this monster?" I said.

I felt some accusatory glares. And ignored them.

He leaned towards me, and a shadow fell over his
face. "A werewolf."

I nodded politely and returned back to our table. I didn't want my soup to get cold and I could practically feel all the knives some of the more superstitious villagers were getting ready to shove into my spine. You don't find many people outside of the cities who like orcs. You don't find anyone who likes the kind that I am. The old man started going off about all the ways to kill a werewolf after that: silver arrows, silver knives, if you cut them in half, or somehow get wolfs bane in them.

AAAAOOOOOOHHH

Silence.

Cold, breathless silence.

AAAAOOOOOHHHAAA

I heard someone whimper from inside the huddle. My own heart began to beat just a little faster. Luce looked at me, eyes blue with concern, mouth no longer smiling.

"We should get upstairs to bed, we have a long day tomorrow." I said. There was no use in staying up and frightening ourselves, just so we can be exhausted for tomorrow. We still had some ways to go up north. Before I stepped in Luce and my room for the night, I noticed Aengel lingering in the hallway.

"Eli," her face was pale.

I went over and gave her my full attention.

She looked up at me, faking confidence. "Do *you* believe the stories? I mean, I could've just been any old wolf just then. I'm just saying."

I shrugged and smiled. Telling her that I was scared too might not have been helpful. "Don't worry, we're safe inside. Get to bed, we have to leave early tomorrow." She nodded and we parted ways. Luce was already passed out on one of the two beds, so I claimed the other and laid myself down.

But I couldn't sleep.

Growing up, I'd fall asleep to the sounds of the moon-soaked forest; wolf howls were just another part of my lullabies. But what was 'lulling' me to sleep that night was not like any wolf call I'd ever heard. For some reason, this one sounded longer, deeper, more full of pain.

It sounded more human.

The howling started farther off farther in the distance, but became louder, longer, and closer as I tossed and turned on the scratchy straw mattress. Luce's snoring couldn't even drown out their howls.

It was calling from the street by the inn.

I heard an ear-splitting scream.

Tearing out of bed and flying down the stairs, my rescue attempt was cut short when I slammed my face into the heavily bolted, reinforced door.

Ow.

I shook off the sharp pain in my nose and took a moment to free the door from the secured frame. Once out into the open night air, I noticed I hadn't dressed for the weather in my rush. Being mid-November, I probably should've remembered shoes. I ignored the stinging cold while I ran towards the screams on the frost covered ground.

There was a man in the middle of the street. The blood coating his crumpled form glinted in the glow of the almost-full moon.

Dead.

Knowing there was nothing more to do for this one, I followed the trail of blood towards the market place in the center of town. My eyes took in my unfamiliar surroundings, ignoring the dark. It was obvious from the wreckage in the square that the beast had been through here. Booths that once held wares were smashed and shops had claw marks decorating the doors. I heard an unholy roar.

Behind me.

I scrambled around and found myself inhaling the hot, sour stench of the beast. A low growl erupted from its throat as it took in the sight of me, as if planning how exactly one eats a creature of my size. His black eyes reached into mine, standing to my height. The scream never made it past my lips.

Move! Move! Good God, Eli!

A howl exploded him my face, snapping me out of my frozen fear and sending me running back toward- well-towards anywhere but near the very hungry werewolf who had just decided I would be his midnight snack. Really though, I should've been an entree.

As fast as I'd like to have thought I could run, I couldn't outrun a werewolf. My feet burned with the freezing cold.

How, Eli? How do you manage to forget shoes at a time like this?

I didn't get far before I was tackled to the ground, slamming my face into the cobblestone.

I went wild.

Screaming, roaring, my legs kicked like they had never kicked before and *I* sank *my* teeth into the thick, wolf fur. The monster let out a yelp of surprise, but that didn't stop me.

Nothing could.

The monster and I tore at each other, both receiving considerable injuries. I managed to keep myself from getting bitten though, because I did not want to be a werewolf. Not. One. Bit. It makes you wonder, though, who was the real monster in that moment? Of course, some of us are only mortal, and the beast threw me on the ground, pinning me to the stone with a clawed foot. In a cry of triumph, he roared his soul out to the moon, then dove in to finish me off.

No, no, no, no- I can't die like this.

In one last attempt for my life, I sank my teeth into his fur-covered ankle.

I bit him before, he really shouldn't have been so surprised.

Sour, hot blood filled my mouth this time, making me choke. The clawed foot had released me to pioneer a new trail of blood leading towards the woods. I rolled over, and coughed up as much of the vile stuff as I could. Most of it ended up on the ground before me, and the rest joined it moments later when I revisited my dinner. Retching pathetically in the middle of the empty street, I cried out for someone, anyone to hear me. But nobody came.

In this town, they seemed to all follow the same protocol: Flee the wolf, save yourself.

Selfish bastards.

Slowly, I made it back to the inn that held my friends. Both arms and my chest were torn up from the monster's claws, and my foot had been stomped on at one point, leaving me with another gash. I was probably going to be more bruise-colored than green by tomorrow. My face was splattered red, tufts of fur stuck in my teeth. I creaked open the door that I had freed earlier and shuffled into the dining room. A few patrons looked up at me in horror. Covered in blood, I hobbled past the astonished stares to the bar. The barkeeper gapped at me like I was the walking dead. I wanted to order myself a tall glass of the hardest drink they had and not hurt all over for just a minute, but instead the words that fell out of my mouth went something like:

"Ya seen my friends?"

Thank goodness I heal fast. I knew I'd probably be in functional shape by the day after tomorrow thanks to my mother's fast-healing blood. There'd be scars, but that's nothing new.

The barkeeper nodded slowly, eyes still wide. He pointed to the door. Nodding my thanks I shuffled back out into the red dawn. I only made it a little ways when someone attack me from the side and attached themselves to me like a small child greeting a long-lost puppy. Aengel. She skirted around me, and took in all the dark blood soaking my torn clothes. There were a few stains on her now too.

"I thought-" She stopped and shook her head. "Well, I'm glad you alive." She gave me a hard smack on the shoulder and turned on her heel before the contact sent her into a vision. "Czara and Luce are over here, we went out after you when Luce woke up and saw you were gone." We rounded the corner, slower than I would've liked. I was pretty scraped up. When the other two saw us, Luce broke into a grin. Czara only looked surprised.

"Looks like your stupidity hasn't killed you yet," she said. Luce said he was glad to see me alive. Noting my change in pace, they all decided I needed some kind of medical treatment. My throat was itching like crazy, so I made little effort to any verbal protests.

"Just get me to the woods," I mumbled. "I can heal myself." My throat was itching before, now it was starting to burn. I coughed. Looking down, I noticed a black ichor staining my arm and dripping from my mouth. *Oh my mother fre-*

"Eli!" Aengel looked at my arm, eyes wide at the black drool. "It's happening."

"What?" I demanded weakly. Luce and Czara rushed to help me stand when I began to sway uncertainly.

"I saw this, I'm so sorry I didn't warn you-"

"It's a little late for apologies, but we appreciate the sentiment," Luce said. The three of them managed to get me back to the inn and up the stairs before I collapsed on my bed, vomiting black. The burning had spread from my throat to my mouth and down my chest like some sort of internal acid fire. I moaned at the pain, despite myself.

"Bloodroot," I whispered through the haze. I don't know if they heard me, so I repeated it with my last sputter of strength. I refused to pass out, but remained foggy. I must've swallowed some blood when I bit the stupid wolf. If that's what was killing me, which made sense, then I knew from my mother's training that bloodroot should do the trick to get it out. Unfortunately bloodroot, handled improperly, could very easily kill me. It was a dangerous toxin that the body has learned to reject pretty effectively, making whatever else inside come out too. If I took too much though, puking wouldn't save me. I had to trust that one of them knew what they were doing.

The vomiting had stopped, but my insides still felt like they were *on fire*. Luce was missing from the room, and the girls were huddled around me, trying to clean the black off and waiting for me to ruin their efforts again. Aengel spoke words of comfort, telling me that everything would be just fine.

Czara worked in silence, doing a stellar job at not letting her worry show. I started to doubt that she actually did care.

Luce came back, producing a small glass vial of a light brown liquid. He pushed past the girls and tried to pour it down my throat. I waved him off weakly and administered the tincture myself. I won't have my dignity lost too. Gagging on the bitterness of the solution, I waited in agony for the poison to hit me. Luckily someone had brought up a bucket. In between, I begged everyone to clear the room. They all followed my orders except for Aengel. I had a feeling she somehow felt responsible for what happened to me. It really wasn't her fault though, Czara was right, it was my own stupidity that had nearly gotten me killed, not her failure to tell me about some vision. How do you tell someone a thing like this anyways?

Hours seemed to pass, and finally my body had nothing left to give. My stomach and throat were sore and burned from all the constant hurling. I prayed that it was enough. My redheaded nurse held the bucket steady and then helped me crawl under the thin covers. The sun had risen and the soft light of morning poured into the room as I was settled in to rest. It was going to be a long day in bed. Tonight was the full moon, and I had a werewolf to kill.

Chapter 14

The entire day was spent eating enough food and water to replace the contents of two stomachs, at least, and sleeping the poison off. I was grateful to the three of them for taking such good care of me, but even more grateful that they didn't, you know, kill me.

That was definitely a plus.

Aengel never left my side, passing the hours talking to me about better times or just sat to be a comforting presence. My insides burned for a while, but gradually the pain lessened until it finally withered back to an itch in my throat. I hated being confined to the bed. I caught my distorted reflection in my spoon when I was eating the soup Czara scored for me from the kitchen. I looked like I had just gone through Hell.

Luce visited me several times throughout the day to check my progress. Apparently he also had some healer training. When he wasn't checking up on me to make sure I wasn't regressing, he was camping out in the girls' room, putting down all the information he remembered about his studies on Mortis so we could narrow down exactly where the animula was, and making a map. Him and his maps, I swear. By mid-afternoon I convinced Aengel to let go of her nurse duties and finally got out of that room to see how Luce's brainstorming session was going. It was time to assume authority again.

He looked up from the papers covering the small wooden desk. "Look who's up," he gave me a light smile.

"I can't stay down for too long,"

"Half orc," he turned to face me full-on. "I have never, *ever*, seen anyone survive anything close to what you just did."

"Uh, thanks."

Well folks, I try. Nothing like trying not to die.

"Really, if the werewolf didn't kill you, whatever happened afterwards should have."

I shrugged. It's not my fault I'm just awesome like that. One thing was nagging at the corner of my mind though. I asked Luce if he knew much on werewolves.

"I'm a Priest of Death- or, I was," he paused considering his clergy status for a moment. "Anyways, you'd think they'd teach us something on the matter."

"Do you know anything about what happens if you swallow their blood?"

He pitched himself back. "Why in Mortis's name would you do a thing like that?"

I gave him a guilty look and tried to force a guilty smile to go along with it.

"No," his eyes widened as far as his face would allow. "You did *not*."

"I did."

Luce rubbed a hand over his face, wiping the sleep from his eyes as if that would change what just happened. I stood there, trying not to think of the worst.

"You're an idiot," he moaned. "Bloodroot isn't going to save you."

"Hey it might though," I retorted. "I got it out pretty quickly." Luce thought for a moment, considering the possibility.

"There's a chance," he said at last. "You've only had the early symptoms, and they've clearly faded. If you don't change tonight, I think you should be safe." I nodded. Tonight was the full moon.

I couldn't help but be a little nervous. Turning into a werewolf wasn't on my list of things to do.

"Meeting in 15 minutes, our room."

"It smells like hurl in there," he complained. I glared at him, my green cheeks flushing as red as green can get.

"Fine, meeting in 15 minutes, *this* room."

He pulled his head back down into his work when I left him to go tell the girls.

Czara wasn't hard to track down and once I found her I found Aengel. It was surprising that the two of them manage to be friends. The barkeeper was able to devote all his attention to the grim-looking half elf. No one else needed his services this early in the day except for only a couple solemn faces occupying scattered stools around the bar. Czara hunched over a line of small glasses while Aengel sat on the stool next to her, smiling when she saw me coming towards them. Czara gave a quiet groan, rubbing her eyes. I told them about the meeting, and 20 minutes later, we were all circled up in the girls' room.

"Okay people," I began. "We have a werewolf to kill. The plan is simple: wolfs bane."

Luce and Czara raised their eyebrow. I could tell Aengel was already trying to guess what this plan could be.

"If we move along, we could find some in the woods. If we don't find any before the sun starts to set, we buy some from the town's healer. Feeding it to him will be too slow, we need to inject it."

"Did you puke out your brain too?" Czara scoffed. "Who's gonna go injecting anything into 300 pounds of monster?"

I gave her a smile. "I guess I have."

Aengel gave Czara a look. "You might be right about his brain."

Luce just smiled at me with a devilish grin. His eyes glinted like he was going to have fun guessing the outcome of this equation. Me + werewolf + terrible plan=?

"If anyone could do this," he slapped my shoulder, "it's Eli."

It took a while to find the wolfs bane, considering Luce and I were the only ones knowledgeable about plants beyond the basics. Czara could recognize them dried, and could probably make something with them, but that was not helpful in the woods. Luce found a patch of it, and we took more than enough to kill a few werewolves. With the help of Czara, who knew more than most people about impromptu alchemy, we were able to extract the plant's toxins and coated one of Czara's daggers with it. By the time we had the poison and the dagger ready, night had fallen and all we could do was wait.

It wasn't long before the howling started.

I stepped out onto the empty street. My only company was the blazing light of the full moon and the sound of someone calling to it, filling the chilled autumn air. I waited. Surprisingly, I wasn't really all that afraid. It was almost like I knew the werewolf coming after me, and I knew what to expect. The knife felt heavy in my hand, but I was ready. Luce, Aengel, and Czara were hidden around the shadows, waiting in case I needed them. Luce had his sword from his priest days, Czara was a warlock, but Aengel only had borrowed dagger. So she's not great in a fight, but she's still a good friend.

A shadow darkened. I saw the beast hiding in the black of a broken shop window, green eyes seething with a hunger for revenge. Peeling away from the shadow, the eerie green eyes skulked towards me, black fur catching the silver moonlight. You had to look for it, but there was a limp in his left leg. I strode towards him, no fear now. We both gained confidence as the distance of cobblestone between us shrunk.

He was the first to strike.

I dodged his claws with elf-like grace and swung the poisoned knife up to meet his over-exposed chest. He wasn't the only one with unnatural speed. My throat burned as I ducked and blocked his attempts.

I smelled blood. Not his, it was human, running down the jagged shards of skull, soaking his once-slick hair.

I'm not a killer.

I very much wanted to *run*. I became sloppy in my dodges, and he gained the upper hand. I didn't want to kill him. As much as I hated him for trying to kill me, I suddenly wasn't too keen on returning the favor. Before I knew it, I was pinned under his massive black paws, gasping for oxygen. He seemed to be studying me with electric green eyes, maybe wondering why I'm not a werewolf too after what happened last night. The knife fell from my hand, and lay on the stone road out of reach. Shaking with the horror of my inevitable and imminent death, I did the only thing I could.

I roared in his demonic, wolf face.

He returned the sound a thousand times louder, shattering my ear drums and sending me into a fit of panic.

Oh God, help me. Please, I'll never cross you again. Oh God, I'll do anything! Not now, don't let me die! Not now!

I closed my eyes. His hot breath stung my face. My last gasps of air in this world would be rancid, reeking werewolf breath. I could feel him open his jagged jaws, preparing for the final attack. Then a great weight fell on top of me, knocking the remaining bits of oxygen right out of my squished lungs, and crushing my ribs.

Luckily I was made of thicker stuff than most.

My eyes shot open when I realized I was still alive, and I saw the lifeless body of the monster laying limp on top of me. Someone, or, several someones, dragged the body off of me. Stunned but relieved, I saw my team hovering over me, making sure I was still alive.

"Hi."

It was the best I could manage at the time.

"You're an idiot," Czara made sure to say before she stormed off back to her bar stool. Luce and Aengel helped me up and we walked back to the inn in silence. Luce seemed less excited about the outcome now. Dark blood covered the front Aengel's dress, but she didn't seem to notice. The knife looked painfully out of place in her delicate, little hands. I let Luce and Aengel go ahead of me back into the tavern, but I didn't manage to make it past the threshold. Very strong, half-elf hands grabbed me by the shirt and yanked me out into the sunless night. Czara's piercing eyes flashed as she grabbed my jaw, pulling my face level with hers.

"Are you *trying* to get yourself killed? Tell me, because I'd *love* to know."

"No! Of course not! I-"

"Shut up, I don't need excuses." Her glare dug into mine. "Every time you have a chance to kill someone you don't." She let go of my face, "Aengel could have died tonight trying to save your sorry, green rear."

"I don't want to kill anyone, I didn't mean for anyone to get hurt. Has that ever occurred to you?"

Pain shot across my face from her bejeweled backhand. Czara was infamous for her rings, and now I realized her purpose for wearing them. "You need to get over yourself, orc. It's in your blood, it's in your nature, and it's in your job description- you either shape up or ship out." My face grew hot and I fought the urge to throw her across the empty street and stomp on her face. Several times. Several.

"Forgive me for having a soul," I spat.

"I'll think about it," she made sure to whip me with her dark hair as she pivoted around, and went inside to be reunited with her bar stool.

For a moment, I considered following her advice, right then and there, to kill without a conscience. Instead, after heaving several deep breaths, I re-entered the tavern and thundered over to her. Grabbing her by the shoulder and forcing her to look in me in the eyes. She let out a gasp of shock.

"I will never lose my soul, I will never lose my conscience, and I will never become like *you*." Without waiting for any response, chin up, I went to my room. Luce was sitting on his bed, pouring over some old maps, when I came in. His head shot up when I slammed the door behind me, almost cracking the wood.

"Hi there," he said.

"Hi." My tone cut the air like a razor.

"Let me guess," he shifted on his bed to face me. "Czara?"

"I could kill that-"

"No, you couldn't."

I looked at him.

"Don't be so surprised, not everyone has it in them to kill. That's a gift, orc, most of us who don't have it secretly wish we did. Pure hearts are rare."

"Pure hearts? I'm not really sure I qualify for having one of those."

He looked at me blankly for a moment. "As much as I'd love to hear whatever past sin you're thinking of right now, I think it's best if you knew that a 'pure heart' is a theological term, and not something that I'd come up with or call anyone on my own before you pour your darkest secrets out to me."

I looked away for a moment, "right."

That night, I laid awake. The sin pricked at the edges of my mind, denying me to sleep. I had to shove the memories away constantly, or else it would've come flooding back and I remember what a terrible son I was. What a terrible person I was.

The first rays of the next day filtered through the dirty linen curtains, signaling the start of a new day. I groaned inwardly that a night had past and I didn't get any sort of sleep. It was the blood that haunted me, and the guilt. Our business was done here, but what happened here was not forgotten. Czara didn't speak a word to me the entire day as we put distance between us and that place.

Chapter 15

The winter sun glared down on us through the bare branches. I didn't notice her riding up next to me until she called out over the hoof beats.

"Hey, how ya feeling?"

"I'm fine." What I didn't want to tell her was that that my gashes from his claws still burned, and I could feel every bruise on this horse. "I never thanked you," I added. "For saving my life and stuff."

"You would have done the same for me." I almost smiled at that. Nobody else seemed to think I had the guts to kill.

At night we heard the howling. Sometimes it got so loud that the forest seemed to shake around us. No one paid any attention to whose turn it was to keep watch, because nobody could sleep with this noise anyways. I had this weird feeling that there was something, somethings, out there in the trees.

When we saw the little lumber village up ahead, Aengel literally laughed with joy. Luce and I shared a knowing look of relief. It was a great feeling to know you don't have to sleep on the ground tonight. Czara only looked slightly relieved. Her personal store of liquor had run out back in the last town a day ago, and she was in dire need of something strong.

It was only a tired old village, where the biggest houses were about two rooms. Everything was rotted or worn out and a certain gloom hung in the air like cobwebs blanketing a once beautiful work of art. We were strangers and held with suspicion. Whispers strung through the air as we rode through. I saw a few of the women hide their eyes when they saw me, even more gave me hateful glares. There was no inn to speak of, either that or they just didn't want us around, so we set up camp on the edge of town and then searched for someplace where we could restock our food supply. Apparently these people only ate what they farmed or hunted, and that seemed to not be doing the trick for most of them by the looks of their sunken faces and bony figures. Desperate not to eat roots, plants, or having to catch our meat, we sent Luce to go bargain with some of the locals. He was eager to see how his haggling skills were, since he'd never bought food at a market before. I found it amazing how much he never experienced during his life in the priesthood. Even I had tried my hand at bargaining, and I lived in the deep woods.

Sometimes gypsies would come through and peddle exotic wares from all across Nyverden. They were a lively people, wearing bright colors with bells sewn into their skirts and shoes. My mother and I never had any gold to buy with, but they accepted herbs and some of our healing services in exchange for some of their foreign teas or a silk scarf for my mother.

About a year ago, a gypsy caravan came through and set up camp for a couple of days a mile away from our hut. There was a woman among them, a girl clear blue eyes that stuck out against her tan skin, who was very sick and very pregnant. In the middle of the night, we heard frantic knocking at our door, and the gypsies begged us to save the dying woman and her unborn child. It was magic that saved her. All elves are born with some sort of magical skill, my mother was a healer but there are skills like control over one of the four elements, lightening, talking to animals. They're born with one skill, but they can learn other magics too, as far as I know. It took well into the next day, and the entire clan waited for the woman outside our hut, refusing to leave their fellow sister. Both the woman and the baby, a little girl with eyes like her mother's, survived. In their gratitude, they made my mother and I adopted members of the clan. They should been coming around this part of the year. I wondered what they'll think when they find out hut abandoned and empty.

The rest of us tried to get some rest at camp, and Aengel set to mending the clothes that the werewolf in the last town had torn up for me. By now, she was becoming a well-practiced seamstress- specializing in half-orc wear. I was talking with the horses when Luce came back with a rotten cabbage and a skinny rabbit carcass. He tossed them onto the blanket Aengel was sitting on next to the fire and threw his hands up.

"Those people are *insufferable*."

Czara looked up from admiring her jewelry on the other side of the fire and raised a dark eyebrow. "Was that the best you could manage?"

"Yeah, it was actually." He let out a frustrated sigh. "At first, nobody would talk to me or even look at me. When I finally did get one to talk, the rest started interrogating me about us and what we're doing here."

"You didn't tell them though, did you?" I said. The last thing we needed was a bunch of villagers getting on our case about trying to kill a Greater Demon.

"No, I just told them we were a group of rangers." He looked at me. "Sorry Eli, but I also had to tell them you were my pet orc."

"Did they believe you?" I tried not to be offended. A lot of country folk would think that orcs are no better than dogs. In all honesty, it did hurt. I'd much rather be a ranger. Rangers were known for being mysterious wanderers of the forest, feared and respected by all, challenged by few.

"Yeah, and then I had to pay an arm and a leg for these two scraps of sh-"

"Okay," Aengel said. "We get the idea." Czara snickered, and then went back to her rings. I found myself glaring at them, remembering the sting as they tore across my face. I was probably just in a bad mood because the villagers think I'm an animal.

Czara was pretty lively at dinner, and I wondered if she had perhaps hit her head or eaten some wrong kind of berry. Or, maybe she was just tired of being alone yet surrounded by people.

Then the howling started.

The very air seemed to vibrate from the chorus. We were close enough to know those weren't wolf howls- they were too human for that. It didn't really matter who was officially on watch duty, we were all huddled around the fire. I noticed Aengel's delicate hands were trembling, so I sat myself on the blanket next to her. Czara and Luce were too nervous to sit, it seemed, so they both paced around the range of the firelight. I had to almost shout it in her ear over the howling.

"You know what happens next?" Maybe she had seen this in one of her visions.

She nodded. "That's what scares me."

Turning my head at the sound of a twig snapping, I realized a pair of electric green eyes had me prisoner to their stare.

Oh. Freaking. No.

Once I saw two eyes, I noticed the hundred more. Instinctively, I pushed Aengel down and shielded her from the gravely snarls coming from the underbrush. She squirmed out from under me in shock before she realized why I had pushed her down. She scrambled back in horror.

"Guys, we've got company..."

Throwing Aengel over my shoulder, I put my trust in my night vision and bolted towards the village. Czara, sprinted ahead, unburdened by 100 pounds of frightened female. Luce who lagged behind with his human legs and lungs, his heaving gasps leaving a trail of sound behind us.

He was fast for a priest, I'll give him that.

The village was silent when we burst into its hold. Luce and I barricaded the entrance with the rotted wood they used for a gate once the last of our terrified horses stormed in, very much aware we didn't have much of a head start. The buildings stood empty and the streets laid hollow. The only sounds that filled the freezing night air were the cries of hundreds of werewolves....

"Oh no," I slid the trembling Aengel off my shoulders. She gave me a look of thanks, unable to make a sound louder than the howling that assaulted our eardrums. The four of us looked around and seemed to all have come to the same conclusion. Creepy, isolated village, hundreds of werewolves, empty houses at night-

"Let's burn it."

I looked over, startled by the sound, only to see Czara staring intensely at the weather-worn houses that now stood expectantly, waiting for its nocturnal residents to return.

"Let's burn the village," she repeated like it was obvious.

"No," I couldn't hide my disgust. "These are innocent people-"

"They're monsters and they *eat* 'innocent people' for breakfast, lunch, and dinner."

"Czara, we can't burn the village."

Luce gave a small giggle, perhaps he was surprised that this was even a legitimate conversation that was actually happening.

Or maybe he was just being Luce.

Aengel pointed out that nobody was actually in the village besides us at the moment, so burning it would be pointless, and, oh yeah, Czara you're a pyromaniac.

Apparently she already knew that, thank you very much you useless weather forecaster.

Luce shrugged. "Screw this, I say we just leave." Aengel nodded, ignoring Czara's silent glare. They all looked to me then, to make the final decision. Burning them all would definitely solve a lot of future problems for this neck of the woods.

"Alright," everyone looked at me, howling drowning out whatever I was about to say. The four of us shared a look. It was time to go.

Within 2 minutes we were riding as fast as our terrified horses could manage in a night thick with dark and noise from a second gate Czara kindly improvised with her purple fire. She got her wish, partially. It was by the grace of someone up there that we made it through the night. We didn't actually see any more werewolves, but we certainly heard them.

Each of us heaved a sigh of relief when the sun rose, shattering the darkness at last. Exhausted and unable to go much further, we found a spot to rest in a clearing and did just so.

Chapter 16

Luce was our navigator. That's why I was slightly surprised when he announced we were now traveling on private property. It was the same forest, same trees, and same animals that scurried underfoot or overhead. Whether it was private or not didn't really seem to matter to me.

"Whose land is it?" Aengel called from the girls' horse. We nonverbally decided that the girls should ride with the girls and the boys would grin and bare it on the other one. Luce rustled around his small space on our over-burdened horse and consulted his map before confirming that it was Lord Dragos of Umbrae Manor. Czara whipped her head around, horror plain on her face.

"You know him?" Luce raised an eyebrow.

"Yeah." She just looked straight ahead again.

I looked at her and sincerely wished I could read minds. Then I thought about it for a second and decided that ignorance just might actually be bliss.

Aengel was the one who couldn't stand the suspense. "How do you know him? Clearly you don't have fond memories, whatever they are."

"He's my brother."

What?

We all stopped our horses. I turned to her and saw she had already composed herself, looking like we had just discussed the imminent rain these dark clouds were promising and not the mention of her brother that had triggered such a reaction,

"Since when did you have a brother?" *Since when was he a lord? Did that mean she was a lady?* I regarded her and decided that it would only be a title anyways.

"Since I was born, he's about five years older than me."

"And he's a lord?" Aengel asked with eyes glinting with curiosity.

"Indeed he is."

"But you and I have known each other for years. You grew up in Shatterpoole, that doesn't make sense."

"You can ask my mother, because apparently it all makes sense to her." I saw a hint of pain pass over her face, but she shoved it back down with all her other emotions before I could really see if it was ever there at all.

"Do you have any other siblings with manors that we should know about?" Luce said.

"Not with manors."

We didn't push her with further questioning even though we all were dying to understand how a girl from the streets of Shatterpoole can have a lord for a brother. And not just any lord. Even I, in my isolated childhood, had heard about Lord Dragos. Rumors, really, but it was said he was more demon than man with black soulless eyes and a heart so cold with cruelty that he'd kill a baby if it so much as irritated him.

"Eli! Duck!"

"Wha-" I jerked myself as close as possible to the horse just in time before an arrow brushed the top of my hair.

"AMBUSH!" I roared. I don't really know if that was the appropriate word, exactly, but it felt right in the moment. Technically we were trespassing- these people had every right to shoot at us.

"Halt!" A voice demanded. Luce and I did our best to steady our horse, but it was difficult given the circumstances. Looking up, I realized that we were completely surrounded by mean-looking men in red uniforms. All but one had arrows trained on each of us. There were six of them. The one without the bow looked like he was in charge, and he stepped forward with an apparent scowl.

"What are you doing on the private lands of the glorious Lord Dragos of Umbrae Manor?" Each word was spoken with a sharp clarity, as if it was vital to him that each sound was accurate as the tip of a razor. Czara answered before I could open my mouth.

"I'm his sister." The soldier scoffed and looked to men to join in his mockery of this foolish half-elf girl sharing a horse with a wild-looking redhead. He quickly silenced them.

"That is a ridiculous lie. The Lord Dragos requires his land be kept untouched by unwelcome feet. The penalty is death". I heard the bows sigh under the pressure of arrows at the ready.

In the heat of a hateful glare, violet fire crackled from Czara's fingertips and singed the hooves of the captain's horse, disintegrating the grass to powdery white ashes. The horse reared and the other guards stared in absolute horror at the smirking half-elf girl. Violet was the color of half-demons, specifically half- greater demons, of which they only knew one other. The head guard steadied his horse and gapped at her like a confused fish.

"Can I go see my big brother now?" With a final shake of her hand, emitting amethyst sparks, Czara regarded the captain with a dangerously playful grin.

"Of course, right this way." His face was scarlet with fear. We rode in mystified silence at the dark haired enigma who rode with amazing dignity for only occupying half a saddle. The other guards rode with their bows at their sides and surrounding us like an official escort. It was weird for me.

We approached the humongous manor house that rose from behind the trees like a fat stone beast covered in dark ivy. I couldn't help but gape at it with my mouth wide open. I had never seen such a large building. It was at least the size of the great cathedral in Shatterpoole, but had the opposite effect on the soul. There was a certain aura to the place that made Aengel and I shiver. Luce sat in his saddle with a studious expression. Czara sighed.

The entry hall was heavily decorated in rich purple and red velvet. I tried to see if the gold and silver detailing was real, but didn't get a chance. We were herded through the hall to an even more extravagant room. It was almost like a throne room with marble columns directing a path from the large doors to the other end of the large room. The lavish ruby carpet trained my gaze to follow it upon a grand stone chair, decorated with intricate designs made up of precious gems and metals. Lounging sideways on the throne was a young man, maybe in his early 20's or late teens. Half of his pale face was hidden by his long black hair that was carelessly swept down. The one eye that we could see was more gold than it was brown, the one ear that we could see pointed to half elf. A cold smirk softened his dark lips. It was a smirk that I was all too familiar with.

"Czara," his eyes flickered with devious delight.

She nodded, "Dragos." I couldn't help but look from one to the other and gaggle at the family resemblance. They both were half elves, obviously, but it was more than that. The ebony hair, the cold expressions paired with malicious smiles, the general supercilious air about them... They were clearly related. Anyone who would have argued otherwise wouldn't be someone worth listening to. He stood and everyone else seemed to shrink. Even I, for once in my life, felt small. It wasn't that he was physically tall, he probably only came up to my chin at best, it was that he had this look about him like he could and should rule the world.

"Did the stars align, or is my beloved sister really here to see her big brother?"

"The stars aligned." She wasn't about to show him any spare kindness.

"You're boring me. Why are you here? Don't you have some powders to mix in that hole you live in?"

"You mean my extremely successful apothecary business in Shatterpoole? No, I've retired for now. We were just passing through and your guards mistook me for a common trespasser."

"They weren't wrong," he scoffed, sitting back down. His blazing gold eyes trained on me. "Who's the orc?" I swallowed.

"My name is Eli."

"That's not a very Orcish name," he studied me.

"No, it's not."

"And you're pretty small even for a half orc."

"And you look pretty girly, even for a half elf." It's true, the man had a neglected pixie-cut and eyeliner.

Just sayin'.

His deathly pale face was suddenly inches from mine. The hairs from my beard were singed by the purple sparks when he grabbed the collar of my filthy shirt and yanked me down to eye-level.

"You have 3 seconds to live, orc."

I shoved him back. The little prince stumbled away from me and I puffed up my chest. "Come at me, bi-"

"Boys!" Czara shoved herself between us. Aengel and Luce gaped in horror at my foolish rashness. Bad move on my part, I know, but he was asking for it. I found Luce behind me, rolling up his sleeves and glaring at the black haired boy, "Dragos, control yourself, and you too Eli. God in heaven, forget about the Valley of Death, I'm in the Valley of Idiots. Luce, back off, you're not helping." Reluctantly, I took a step away from the siblings and Luce followed in suit.

Dragos returned our glares tenfold. "Why are you helping them, Czara? I know what you're doing here." He straightened himself out a bit and added, "Do they even know?"

I looked at Czara and found her cheeks flushed with the red of a thousand embarrassments, fears, and horrors. I couldn't help but wonder out loud. "What is he talking about?"

He smiled.

"You haven't." His whole demeanor changed and he strolled back to his throne. "I'm willing to let you all stay for dinner, but that's all. Actually." he turned back to us. "I'll give you two horses so my sister can retain the *little* left of her dignity and Eli's poor animal doesn't have to bear such weight." I struggled not to respond.

"What are you up to?" Czara wasn't the only suspicious one. He was clearly playing at something and it was humor at her expense.

"Is it *wrong* to invite my little sister and her friends to dinner? Come, come now, sister, you shall *have* to clean up." He regarded us, eyes lingering on our blushing Aengel. "Your friends too," he added with an extra devious smile.

This was the first time I saw Czara truly helpless.

Servants led us to rooms where we were able to wash up and rest before Dragos's dinner. As hungry as I was, and believe me, I was hungry, this was one meal I was not looking forward to. Whatever it was the Dragos was doing, I had to assume the worst. The very water I was splashing on my face could've been poisoned. Maybe there was even an assassin hiding in the wardrobe. No, no one in there. Maybe I was just being paranoid. Maybe that was justified given the circumstances.

Knock, knock, knock, kno-

I tore open the door.

"Hello?"

Aengel stood there, her face finally free of the shade of dirt and her hair tamed into a simple low-bun, not wild and all over the place like it usually is. She looked pretty with it wild, but having it pulled up and back looked... elegant. Yes, she looked elegant.

"Can I come in?"

"Oh, yeah, sure."

She scurried past me and I made sure to close the door behind her. I noticed her fingernail beds were raw and bleed from nervous picking.

"You good?" I grabbed a hand to assess the damage. I had some antiseptic to put on the open cuts to avoid infection.

She slid her hand away, and then I remembered why she avoids contact. "Yeah, I'm good. I was just wondering what you think about this whole thing."

I thought for a moment. "Well, I was sleeping on tree roots last night, before that I was almost turned into a werewolf, and now I'm about to have dinner with one of the most notorious lords in all of Nyverden who happens to be Czara's brother. It's a crazy world out there, but I do agree, this is definitely one of the weirder situations we've been in."

'Did *you* know they were siblings?"

I shook my head. How could anyone have known? Czara is as much of an open book as the Queen's inner sanctum. Before we could say anything else, a servant, who reminded me of a lizard for some reason, stuck his head into the room and summoned us for dinner.

Chapter 17

Luce and Czara were already assembled outside the massive door to the dining hall by the time Aengel and I came down. The doors opened and I'm not really sure what exactly happened. What I do know is that Czara looked like all the sick, black pain in the world just drained away every smile, laugh, and happiness she had ever known.

"*You.*"

Seated at the head of the food laden table next to a smirking Dragos, was a man I instantly recognized even without his mask. He was a man whose very name blotted out the sun. He was a man that silenced laughter, and a man that laughed in the silence in death.

Missi Mortis.

There was no doubt in my mind that Dragos was his son, they could've been twins, save Mortis's wider face and less feminine hair. It was his eyes too, though. They weren't just gold in color, the pigment flickered as if it was truly the fires of Hell.

They do say that eyes are the windows to the soul.

"My Czara," I shivered at his smile. "You didn't say you were bringing friends home for dinner." The supercilious smile that tugged at his lips was one that I had seen before.

Oh. My. Saints.

Czara Mortis.

"You wouldn't know anything about my *friends*," she spat with obvious hate. She looked like she was struggling for air. I found my own hands shaking. She managed to regain some control of herself and speak.

"Never, not *once* did you contact me. *Not once.*" The more she spoke, the more her confidence returned.

Storming towards him, every feeling of abandonment, hate, and pain surfaced.

"Thirty years! Never did you so much as *acknowledge* my *existence*! How *DARE* you call me yours! I am not your daughter."

"My darling girl," he picked casually at a hangnail. "I had no idea that gentle elf wench instilled so many family values into you." He looked back at her, "neither of us were much for them."

"I instilled my *own* values", Czara growled through her teeth. He laughed as if a plan had finally come together and the good news just fell in his lap. The fire at her hands sparked a violent shade of purple.

"I'm tired of this family reunion," she said. "The time for familial sympathies is expired. I no longer want you alive, so I am going to kill you. If you and your elven skank, Rhone, taught me anything as parents; it's that I can and will do whatever the hell I want."

Luce, Aengel, and I were too horribly shocked by the whole situation to do anything but gape. I wanted so much to find a way to help her, if I only knew how. The most I could do was stand behind her and cheer her on underneath the chains of shock and fear that kept me silent and motionless.

She threw a ball of violet flames at him, missing on purpose.

"I can add 'Bastard of a Father' on your grave rock when we drag your mutilated corpse from this hall and dump you in a shallow grave."

He smiled and rose from his place at the ornately decorated table. His tall statue radiated power and control. The Prince of Death.

Her father.

"I'd need a soul for you to kill me."

Czara screamed in frustration and spewed purple fire onto her immortal father. He stood there looking mildly annoyed as she desperately tried to roast him. Realizing her attempts were useless, she stopped. Her ragged breathing shook the toxic air.

"Well," Mortis said. "That was mature."

I finally stepped forward. "Let's go guys, we've overstayed our welcome." *Among other things...*

"You're not going anywhere, *Eli*," Mortis hissed my name like it was hot metal shoved in his mouth. "I know exactly what you're looking for. The animula? You'll never find it, not while I'm alive." He strode towards me, malice blazing in his smile. "I have purposes for you yet."

We stood face to face- me and my demon. I dared not breathe. I could feel every inch between us screaming with danger.

"Leave me alone," I whispered.

He smiled.

"Never."

Summoning all the courage I didn't have, I went to take another step towards him. Nothing. I tugged harder for my foot. No, nothing. My feet were mercilessly stuck to the stone floor.

"*Let me go!*" I roared. My friends suddenly found themselves stuck the same way, panic rippling across the room.

"Release us!" Aengel's cheeks were flushed bright red. Luce was clearly trying not to freak, but his eyes completely failed at hiding what we were all feeling. Czara looked beyond defeated. Our other limbs were fine, it was our feet that were welded to the stone floor. Mortis weaved between the four of us, dodging Czara's furious attempts at attacking him from her glued place.

"You *will* join us for dinner." We found ourselves all shuffling to different places at the table. I tried to resist with all my strength, knocking over chairs and clawing at everything and anything to keep from obeying my treacherous feet. Luce even managed to throw one of the china plates from the decorated table at Mortis but missed by inches. There was no stopping him. Dragged to our places despite our best efforts, none of us were able to even acknowledge the incredible feast laid before us. There was nothing any of us could think to say that would really help, and this was no time for food. Luce looked like he was about to throw up all over the table.

"You're a sick bastard."

"I know." Mortis didn't miss a beat

"What do you want with us?" I said. "If you're going to kill us, do it now."

"And miss all this fun?" he laughed. "No, no. I'm rather enjoying this little family dinner. Besides, killing you, Eli, would be of no use to me." Then he looked at Aengel and Luce, finally his eyes resting on Czara. "I could do without them though."

"If you kill them, you'll have to kill me too."

Mortis laughed. "Of course." He said it like we both knew I was lying, which I wasn't. Or, I thought I wasn't. As poorly as we knew each other, I had become fairly close with the three of them and didn't want them dead, at least. Maybe sometimes, but not actually.

The four of us sat there while Dragos and Mortis ate the fat meat pies and the fabulously adorned roasted peacock. I wanted *them* dead. Aengel and I caught each other's gaze for a moment and I tried to comfort her telepathically. Pathetic, I know, but it was all I could do. Luce and Czara were fighting the silence while Aengel and I were almost taking comfort in the motionlessness of it. Finally Luce gave in.

"All my life I've lived as a priest at your temple, and I can't even tell you how weird it is to being seeing you in the flesh. I expected someone much more intimidating. Oh well, I guess. Can't have it all."

Mortis raised a dark eyebrow and the two men paused their dinner. *No Luce, just shut up please, you're not helping.*

"Am I not frightening enough for you? Priest? You're not really even a priest anymore. I know all about *you*, Lucifer."

The blonde boy turned a horrible shade red.

"What do *you* know about *me*?"

"I know everything about my priests." Personally, I was surprised a demon of Mortis's status would bother with any of his subordinates.

"Oh really?"

"Of course," Mortis said. Clearly he wasn't impressed.

All the while I couldn't help but wonder how much I didn't know about all the people sitting at that table. I had no idea "Luce" was just a nickname. Everyone has secrets, everyone has a past. But I really kicked myself for not realizing earlier that Czara was Mortis's daughter. I mean, I knew she was of part demon, but not *that* demon.

I noticed Dragos staring at Aengel again, like when he was in the throne room.

"Find something you like?" she shot at him. No matter who, what, or when, she knew how to handle herself. He smiled. He and his demon father shared a knowing look.

Chills ran down my spine.

"I'm done with dinner," Mortis stood. "Dragos, you know what to do." The demon walked out of the hall, reminding me that the only exit was beyond my desperate reach. Dragos hardly waited for his dark father to fully disappear from view before standing and addressing his dinner guests/prisoners.

"Ladies, gentlemen, orc," a low growl boiled in my throat- he ignored me and continued. "Some of you will be able to walk away from this manor, some will not." He was sure to call this place a "manor", I could tell.

"None of us can go anywhere like *this*, imbecile." Czara spat.

"Hush, sister. You're annoying me. And if you annoy me, then you can't play with me and my friends."

I shuddered.

"Who said we want to play with you?" Luce gave him an inquisitive look.

Aengel and I couldn't hold back giggles, but they were quickly cut off when Dragos spoke. Fury clear in his voice.

"You play or you die. If you don't want to play, that only makes things simpler for everyone." He flicked back his impressive black hair. "But boring. Here are the rules: each of you must pick a door, but none of you can go in the same door. Once I leave this room, your legs will be unbounded and you may go about as you wish for as long as you want in this room only if you eventually choose a door."

His footfalls echoed like thunder on the stone floor when he paraded out the hall.

The four of us looked at each other, unsure of what to do. A warm wind seemed to wrap around my feet, but I had little time to enjoy it before four strange doors appeared side by side on the far wall. The first door was made of gold, jewels encrusted in elaborate patterns on its face. On its left was a silver door with glittering sapphires decorating its surface. The third was a bronze door, scenes of a summer hunt crowding it from top to bottom. Giving off a strange air, the final door was a simple wooden one that I could've very easily seen in Shatterpoole or any other town in Nyverden.

I stood.

"If we can't think of anything better, I suggest we start picking who's going through which door soon."

"Let's think about this logically," Aengel said. "We can't just go through doors without considering where they'll go."

"What choice do we have?" Luce looked disdainfully at the four doors watching us from the far wall.

"We could just not pick a door, nobody said we had to do this," Czara flopped her boots on the table, making clear dirt marks on the fine fabric tablecloth.

"I think since death is the only other option, it sounds like a pretty forced issue we have here," Aengel said.

Then suddenly I had an idea. "You can see into the future, can't you?"

"I'm an aspicien, I certainly hope I can manage that." She was trying too hard to keep calm, making herself more panicked.

"It's going to be okay," I promised before I said anything else. "Why don't you look into my future and see if we can get an idea about these doors here." She nodded and straightened herself of. Luce and Czara watched as she and I met at the end of the table by the doors. She took my hand carefully, as if I was a delicate newborn rabbit.

"I think it would be best if we both kneeled," she said shyly. I recalled her episode by the docks when she almost fainted. We sank to the floor, and she took a deep breath before closing her eyes. Her thin shoulders shook for a terrifying second and her wildly topped head jerked. I wasn't sure whether to be in awe of her extraordinary power, or afraid. She pitched back and cried out, sending Luce and Czara running towards us. They only found themselves helpless in watching the little redhead contort under her power, twisting this way and that, gripping my trembling hand all the while.

Pale, soaked with sweat and tears, she opened her eyes.

"I know which door you shouldn't go through."

Chapter 18

"Don't go through the gold one," she urged me. "Please, promise you won't." I took her by the hands and helped her to her shaky feet. I dared not let go in fear of her collapsing from the strain. Luce and Czara helped me steady her and get her into a chair.

"Why?" I said.

"I can't say for sure," she pushed her dampened hair out of her face. "When I have visions it's like a bunch of images all flashing before me at once, I can only catch glimpses of each moment before the others overwhelm me."

"What did you see?" Czara pushed.

She drifted her bright green eyes to me. "I saw you die." Her pale pink lip trembled.

Despite myself, I shuddered and couldn't help the ball of panic sink in my stomach or the pagan drumbeat of my heart.

"How?" Leave it to Luce to ask a thing like that at a moment like this.

"I killed you." She sobbed, throwing her face into her shaking hands. I wouldn't have asked her to do this if I knew it would make her cry.

Czara looked at me, shock clear on her face. "What?"

"I don't know, all I saw was me sticking a sword right through him and he falls to the ground in a bloody, green heap." Her voice cracked on the last word.

"Okay," I said. "So I won't go through the gold door." Czara's hopeless laugh echoed through the hall.

"I hope you're enjoying the show!" She screamed at the ceiling. Shaking her dark head, she could only laugh.

That's when I noticed the fog.

Or maybe it wasn't fog, maybe it was some kind of gas. I don't really know. All I knew was that the floor started to evaporate into a cold, gray mist, making me choke on the fumes. We had to clear out, and fast.

"Get through the doors!" In an instant I was about to throw myself through the wooden door when I saw Aengel on her knees, gasping for oxygen and still weak from the vision. Czara and Luce had already gone through the silver and bronze doors. Without thinking, I hauled the redhead over my shoulder and burst through my wooden exit. Yes, I broke a rule, but does that really matter when the game is twisted anyways?

I wasn't able to stop my momentum until she and I were well past the threshold. The first thing I noticed was the cold. Thank goodness I remembered my boots this time. I was suddenly aware that I was up to my shins in glittering, white snow. My pant legs began to feel wet, my body heat melting the snow stuck to me. Aengel cried out and shifted on my shoulder, uncomfortable with so much physical contact. Then she noticed the snow, and quit squirming so hard.

"You know," I called over the wind. "I don't mind carrying you."

She wiggled her toes in her thin leather slippers. "No, I can walk."

"I don't think-"

She didn't wait for me to finish before squirming off my shoulder into the snow. For one, frozen moment she stood there, letting the cold sink in.

"Never mind," she stammered. I threw her over my shoulder again and stomped on through the drifts to find some shelter. The snowflakes were coming down frantically, making it difficult to see too far ahead.

Where do you suppose we are?

"It looks like Franken, if I ever saw it," Aengel said. I hadn't realized I'd said anything out loud. She had nothing on but her green, rough cotton dress and wool stockings with worn leather shoes. The only thing keeping her warm was her long, wild hair. I felt sorry for her, but I had the minimum on too. Selfishly, the real reason I wanted to carry her was not because I didn't want her walking in the snow, but because she was like a human blanket.

We trudged along for what seemed like forever, the tiny snowflakes stinging my exposed skin. We came into an area that seemed like rocks were under the piles of snow. Jagged boulders jutted out of the white, and it wasn't too long before Aengel spotted an abandoned fox den. I slid her through the opening before squeezing myself in. I give the fox who built it props for the space. I could sit up pretty easily, and laid down without too my issue. It was like the pantry back at the Blue Bear, but on its side. No food though, just dirt and roots poking through the walls. Distantly, I realized my feet were quite numb, and now were stinging like a thousand little knives as the feeling came rushing back. It took me a minute to pull of my soaking boots because the cold *hurt*, but once off, I furiously rubbed the feeling back into my feet.

"How are you?" I noticed Aengel curling herself into the smallest ball imaginable to keep warm.

"I'm a little *frozen*."

I laughed, sending billowy clouds of vapor into the air around me. "I've definitely been warmer."

"I thought orcs couldn't feel cold."

If only.

"Who told you that?"

"It's a rumor." She brushed the hair away from her face and tried to nestle down into the packed dirt floor. I sat there for a moment, wondering what on earth we were going to do next. Who knows what kind of games Mortis was playing when he set up those doors. Clearly he was trying to split us up, but I knew he needed me too much to kill me. There had to be some sort of purpose to this door, I just hadn't figured it out yet.

It was so *cold*.

Wherever we were, we couldn't stay still for long. I knew we had to keep moving and find some sort of civilization before we froze or starved to death. We very well couldn't stay in the fox den for the rest of our lives, however long they were destined to be. Then again, destiny said I'd go through the gold door and look at me now.

"We should rest and then set off and look for help," I said.

"How? We can't go around in the snow like this. We'll freeze."

"We'll manage."

Exhausted from a full day of adventure and an unplanned winter walk, the dirt floor was almost comfortable. I curled up on the other side of the den, away from Aengel. Shivering, I was afraid to go to sleep in fear that I'd never wake up again. Say I froze to death in my sleep? Say my feet turn blue and chip right off my legs? Eventually, my eyelids forced themselves shut and I found myself back in the spring time in the woods, helping my mother stitch up a puppy who was less than cautious when it came to thorn bushes.

Chapter 19

My nose tickled and I felt something soft brush against my cold cheek.

"Gah! Aengel!" I scrambled away from her seconds before she woke up and did the same.

"Eli! What the hell?"

"Me?! We must have moved around in our sleep! No offense, but no thanks."

Her face reddened and she puffed up like an angry peacock. "Likewise, half orc." She straightened her dress and sat as far away from me as she could manage in the small space. I broke the awkward silence and quickly suggested we keep moving. As soon as I saw her face in response, I realized that that would actually mean *more* awkwardness because I had to carry her through the snow.

"We can't stay here, and look, the snow's stopped," I pointed to the small opening leading into the den.

"Fine," she grumbled.

I noticed she was shivering when she climbed out of the den. My body had long since accepted the cold, although it was not numb to it. Once outside, I picked her up and slung her over my shoulder, and we kept going in the direction we were headed last night. With the blizzard gone and not blocking my view, I could see that the land was rocky, with large, sharp boulders breaking up the landscape, and covered in shimmering snow. The boulders made it difficult to see too far into the distance, but as far as I could tell, it was a wasteland.

Aengel was right, maybe this is Franken.

I stomped through the snow, often taking breaks on the rocks that provided refuge from the white ground. Working so hard to plow through the land and carrying a 110 lbs. girl kept me from getting too cold. In fact, I almost felt warm a couple times. I don't think we even made it a mile before I called for another rest. I pulled much needed oxygen into my lungs and cringed as my stomach complained of utter emptiness. I couldn't remember the last thing I had to eat. At least the snow provided us with all the cold water we needed. And much, much more.

Aengel was about to open her mouth when we heard bells.

Jingling, Christmas bells.

We shared a look mixed with confusion and then desperate hope that whoever the owner of these bells was might be our savior from this frozen Hell.

A simple wooden sleigh came into view. At first, I could only see the sleigh and the black horse that was pulling it, but soon I saw a man cozied down with a plethora of blankets holding the reins. Wasting no time, I waved to him frantically and he pulled over to us on our slate island.

"Hello! I was wondering if you could give us a ride."

He looked about early 20's with his black hair in a flo and icy blue eyes. His skin was as pale as the snow around us. Nestled in his warm coat and blankets, he looked at us with amusement. Something about him sparked with familiarity.

"What on this white, frozen earth are ya doing here?"

"It's a long story," I said. I had no intention of telling him very much about how we managed to get in the middle of a snow desert with nothing but our autumn clothes on. I looked at him for a second, a memory tugging at the back of my brain. This guy looked so familiar.

"Well, good thing I found ya both, or I'd be finding some meaty popsicles."

Then it hit me: the Antimarx's dungeon. It was my old cellmate!

"Hey! It's you!" I was suddenly even more excited to see him. Aengel looked at me and then to him, and then to me again.

He nodded. "Fate has an interesting sense of humor." He motioned for us to get in the sleigh, and for the first time in a long time, I felt cozy.

"So," Aengel said, pulling a fur blanket over herself. "How exactly do you two know each other?"

"We were cellmates back at the Antimarx's." I tried to ignore the awful memories of rancid darkness. It still gave me chills. When I asked him how he got out, he just told me that some secrets were best left where they lie.

Lie indeed.

"Ya know, Eli, it's great seeing you and all, but don't think for one more second that this ride is for free."

Aengel and I looked at him curiously.

"A favor for a favor."

"What exactly do you have in mind?" I said.

He looked at me and smiled. "I don't know, but I'll think of something."

This made me nervous.

We rode the rest of the way in silence. The only sound was of the wooden runners cutting through the snow and those bells.

After about 15 minutes of riding and getting warm in the borrowed blankets, a very interesting sight came into view. I didn't believe my eyes at first, or even as we got closer, but whether or not I believed it, a castle of ice laid before us. The closest to a castle I'd ever seen was the Antimarx manor, but this was at least 5 times the size. It wasn't just the colossal size that amazed me, it was that the entire structure was one, big ice sculpture. It was beautiful.

"Here we are," my cellmate pulled up to the grand, ice door. The three of us piled out of the sleigh onto the packed snow. I'm sure Aengel shared in my gratefulness for not having to carry her through the snow ever again. My cellmate led the way up the steps. Aengel and I trailed behind, trying not to slip. The ice castle was gorgeous, but not practical.

"You live here?" Aengel shouted up to him.

"I stay here."

What is that supposed to mean?

"Hey, I never got your name." I said once we reached to door.

He turned to me, eyes icy with delight. "You've never needed to."

Nice.

We followed him down the grand hall and up a magnificent staircase. Upstairs there was a hallway of doors, the walls were made of a cloudier sort of ice, making the walls impossible to see through.

"This one's your room," he said to Aengel. Then he pointed to the door next to it and said it was mine. "Dinner's in a half hour, I'll come collect you." And then he disappeared back down the stairs. The redhead and I shared a long, concerned look before going into our respective rooms. This whole thing was starting to smell fishy. He comes and rescues us, for which I am grateful, and then leaves us separated in some random ice castle.

I couldn't believe my eyes when I opened the door. My room was something I'd expect for a king, at *least*. The bed was massive, with four posts and a thick red velvet canopy- I later discovered there was a string I could pull to get a thick curtain to surround it. There was a large, stone fireplace in use, giving the room warmth and light. I was actually surprised that the room wasn't melting. My guess what that some kind of magic was at work here. Thick, fur carpets covered the ground, making walking not such a risky concentration exercise. After standing in front of the fire for a good ten minutes, I noticed some clothes laid out on the bed. There were thick, black pants with suspenders, a phenomenon I had only heard about, a black shirt/coat-sort that went down to my knees and had two rows of buttons going down it. I left my old boots to dry by the fire, and hurried to pull on the tall new ones that were waiting for me with the rest of my mysterious new clothes.

Taking a damp wash cloth, the full extent of my filth was obvious as the white cloth quickly turned brown. Looking in the full-length mirror next to the basin, I was almost startled at the sight. The new, shiny boots stood out against my tattered, filthy clothes and my dirt-covered skin. My ebony hair was wild making me look like a rabid orc. After a long time cleaning up, my skin gleamed deep green once again, and I managed to get my hair to fluff up top and slick on the sides like it used to. Once in my new clothes, I looked pretty darn sharp and ready for winter.

I reveled in the clean warmth.

I sat by the fire and wondered about Luce and Czara while I waited for my cellmate to come. I felt guilty about being so comfy while I couldn't help but guess if those other two were still alive.

Two steady knocks sounded at my door, I opened it to find my cellmate and Aengel waiting in the hallway. I couldn't help it- she looked beautiful. Dressed in a full-length white, lace gown with her hair twisted up into a crimson bun, she looked like a queen. That's all I could think of as her brilliant green eyes noted my own polished appearance.

My cellmate let out a low snicker, and started walking down the hallway. Both us of scrambled to follow, trying to forget that moment just then. We couldn't afford to lose focus in a castle made of ice.

Dinner was a feast much like the one at the Mortis manor. The strange thing was, my cellmate- whom I guessed was the master of the house- didn't sit at the head of the table. I wanted to ask about it, but didn't really know how to address a guy who wouldn't even give me his name. Aengel was less reserved when it came to formalities.

"Who's sitting at the head of the table?" Her voice seemed to echo through the ice walls.

"The lord of the house," my cellmate said through sips from his fancy silver chalice.

"And who might that be, exactly?" she said. I noticed she hadn't touched her pile of food, unlike me. She must've been just as starving as I was. She was suspicious. Let's chalk that one up to growing up in Shatterpoole.

My mysterious cellmate gave her a smile that was meant to falsely reassure her, but she didn't take the bait.

"I don't mean to be rude," she said. "But I'd at least like to know the name of the man whose house I'm in." That seemed reasonable, I'd say.

"His name is Lord Yaroslavek of the House of Vadim. He'll be joining us later, do you think you can hold yer patience 'til then?"

She looked at him with hard eyes.

"I can't make many promises."

"Well," I said, breaking both of their glares. "Whoever he is, I'm grateful for his hospitality." I stressed the word "grateful", and made a show of glancing at my redheaded companion. There was no need to be so rude to our hosts.

I was tempted to ask again for my cellmate's name, but my tact stopped me, so instead I asked about the architecture of the castle. Dinner was finished with casual conversation about ice and the confirmation that this was, indeed, Franken. Aengel beamed a triumphant look, as if she knew she was right about that all along. After dinner, our host excused himself and wished us a good night. We both decided to return to our rooms and get some much-needed sleep.

When I walked in my room, I was surprised to find a large wooden trunk at the foot of the large bed.

Where's all this stuff coming from? I haven't seen one servant.

It's true. The only people I'd seen since we got here were Aengel and my cellmate. Curious but cautious, I opened the trunk to find it stuffed neatly with fine winter clothes that were all- shockingly- my size. As if the fact that clothes were appearing in my room wasn't strange enough, the fact that they all seemed to be tailored to me was enough to get me creeped out when I should have been grateful. I was already getting that uneasy vibe from dinner, but now I was just downright paranoid. Who was this guy? Whose house is this? And why the heck am I here? As nervous as I was, my body was determined to sleep. I had been up and moving for too long at this point and I was just done. I ignored my cautious nerves and pulled a cozy set of flannel pajamas out of the trunk. I thought only kings could wear pajamas like these. Every noise made me jump and grab the fire poker while I washed up and pulled on the softest material I'd ever worn in working memory. I flopped into bed and laid there, taking in the vastness of the room and its echoing sounds. The wind whirling outside seemed to be amplified and the crackling of the fire became unfriendly. I tried every which way to lie myself in the bed, but nothing seemed to take away the dark empty feeling the room was giving off.

There was a soft knocking at my door that snap me out of the panicked daze I was in. I heaved a sigh and rolled out of the nice, warm bed to answer it. I opened the door and should've been less surprised.

"I can't sleep," Aengel stated. "The room's too big."

And this constitutes my involvement how?

"Me neither," was all I said.

"Can I sleep in your room?"

I raised an eyebrow, but said sure. Part of me wanted to help her out, but mostly I just wanted her around to make the room less empty so I could actually sleep and not worry about the hollowness that the room seemed to ooze with. The other part of me was screaming "NO WAY!" All things considered.

I may have been raised in the forest, but I know what's proper and what's not. I even had some religion on this thanks to Father Elijah. Not that my race constituted to me the full benefits of faith. I let her take the bed while I snagged a blanket and slept by the fire. Hearing her steady breathing quieted the howl of the wind, and the sound of her rustling the sheets make the fire feel that much warmer. A room can be as comfortable or as rich as it wants, without people to fill it it's just an empty room.

Chapter 20

It was the sunlight that woke me. I was dreaming of my skin being fair instead of green, my teeth without fangs, and no scars decorating my body. I dreamt I was as human as Aengel and Luce. They don't know how lucky they are. I sat up, pulling the knitted blanket around me, and noticed that someone must've come in and tended the fire. It glowed lowly, giving just enough warmth and light for a slow morning. I stood up and saw that Aengel was still curled up in the middle of the bed. She really did look like an angel with her hair spread out like that and her face so peaceful. I realized I probably shouldn't be looking at her while she's sleeping like that, so I turned away and decided to sit by the fire until she woke up. I would've gotten washed and dressed, but I was afraid she'd wake up at a bad time. The whole situation was unorthodox as is. I watched the flames of the fire flick up and down while I wondered what it'd be like to be human. I wondered what I'd look like, if I'd still be so massively tall. I heard rustling from the bed and saw Aengel sitting up. Confused and groggy, she looked at me as if she had no clue why I was there. She suddenly remembered and wished me a good morning.

"Good morning," I tried to keep my eyes on the fire as much as possible. She slid out of the bed, careful to keep her nightgown modestly over her legs.

"I'm gonna go get dressed."

"Okay," I called after her. Once she was gone, I surveyed the contents of the trunk and found some more black pants with those suspenders, a white cotton button-up, and then a smart black waist coat. If only my mother could've seen me. I stopped. If only she could see me. I pulled on the clothes, but was met with dismay when I looked in the mirror. The only thoughts running through my mind was that I looked like a grizzly bear in a suit. It had the same effect as a dog in a dress. I was about to change back into my old clothes, however tattered they may have been, but I heard knocking at my door and felt obligated to answer it.

"I found these in my room, I think they're for both of us," Aengel held out a tray of pastries with two mugs of hot chocolate. I let her in, and wondered out loud who was leaving these things for us.

"I don't know," she looked at me. "But I guess it'd be rude to question it."

I remembered last night and gave a little laugh. "I didn't know you were into manners."

"I know." She plopped down by the fire, carefully arranging her white silk skirts around her on the rug. I wondered if whoever it was leaving the clothes and the food thought white was her color or was playing off her name. We ate our breakfast without much interruption. None, in fact. Neither of us had seen any other signs of life besides each other since dinner last night. We stayed by the fire for a bit, but curiosity took over and I suggested we go exploring. It's not every day you stay in a castle of ice.

This time, we both had on winter boots, making walking on the ice floor easier, but still difficult. I made a show of trying to skate down the long hallway and Aengel couldn't help but laugh at my painful attempts. *Painful* attempts. After sliding down a few hallways, we came to a dead end with a large wooden door. I thought this was weird, considering the rest of the house was all ice. It seemed terribly out of place.

"Let's open it," I heard myself say.

Aengel looked at me. "What if someone's in there or something?"

"Then we apologize politely, I guess." Before further discussion, hesitation, or just general never-minding's, I pushed it open.

The result was slightly disappointing.

For me, anyways. Aengel seemed to be having a different reaction. It was just a large wooden room with a stage at the end of it. In the middle of the stage was a delicate looking heap of material. Aengel rushed over to it, and gingerly lifted up the little dress that had the shortest, puffiest skirt I'd ever seen. She knelt and picked up the slippers that laid next to her.

"Um," I said from the door. "What are you doing?"

"Have you ever heard of ballet, orc?"

Bal-eh-what? And, it's half orc.

"No."

"Well," she smiled smugly at me. "That's not terribly shocking."

I scoffed. "If it's one of those dancing things, you can put me down for violently uneducated and I have no intention of changing that." I turned to walk out, but she didn't follow me.

"Well, come on."

She sighed, letting go of the dress.

"There you two are, I've been looking all over for you." I turned to see my cell mate standing in the hallway with a stupid smile on his face. Suddenly I felt like a mouse who'd just eaten poisoned cheese.

"I see you've gotten some exploring in, how about some lunch?"

Aengel reluctantly left the stage and we followed him down the stairs back to the dining room where lunch was already laid out for us. I tried to search around for anyone who might have laid it out, or just anyone else in general.

"Where are the servants?" I said as we sat down.

"Servants?"

"Yeah, who brought the clothes and the food?" Aengel blinked her big green eyes at him.

"Oh, those are the auxiliatrix. You can't see them, but don't worry, they're there."

"What are they?" I'd never heard of an auxila-whatsa-who.

"Nobody knows what they actually look like except the master of the house, I believe. He discovered them years ago and brought them to work here."

"Like slaves?" Aengel raised a disapproving eyebrow. Slavery is illegal in Nyverden.

"Yes," our host looked disturbingly unconcerned. We were in Franken now.

"Eli, the master of the house would like to speak to you after lunch." My cellmate continued without missing a beat.

"Not Aengel?"

"No."

We shared a concerned look.

"Why not?"

"Master's orders," he ignored my reluctance, as if I was overjoyed to meet the mysterious, and possibly dangerous, master of the house.

After lunch, I nodded an uncertain goodbye to my one friend and trailed after my cellmate down an unfamiliar hallway. My hands were sweaty and the ice gave off more cold than I had noticed earlier. We came before a large door, decorated with carvings of wintertime. My cellmate knocked confidently on the ice.

"Enter!"

The door opened, revealing a large man with shocking gold hair crowning his head and beard. He stood up and gave me a smile.

"Eli Krillson, it is an honor." He came over to shake my hand. "You must forgive my absence, I have been looking forward to meeting you."

"It's all good," was what I managed to say.

"You must be wondering how you got here. Of all the places, why would Mortis send you here?"

"I assumed he didn't know we'd be rescued, but frozen wasteland seems his style." That was the only theory I had.

The large man laughed. "Certainly, certainly. But no, it was I who sent you here. I intercepted the signal from the door you took back at the Mortis house and sent you here. Unfortunately, it was more difficult than I thought, and you ended up some miles away from us."

"Why did you bring me here?"

"Right to business then, I see." he said. I noticed my cellmate had disappeared.

Fabulous.

"You realize how valuable you are, don't you?" he said.

"I've been told." Where was all this going?

"And certainly you wouldn't want to waste your power raising evil with a demon like Mortis?"

"I'd die first."

"Good, good. I believe I have a solution for your powers not to go to waste."

I raised an eyebrow. "I don't follow."

"You know that you have the power to raise Mortis's demon army, but did you know that only you can control it?"

"What about the people who control me?" I stepped back a little from the large man.

He laughed a low, deep laugh. "Who said anything about controlling you, my dear boy? No, no. Think of it more as a partnership. What would *you* do with a demon army? Really?"

"I can be creative."

"No one's doubting that," he motioned me over to his desk. A map of the known world laid on it, and I took a moment to marvel at how much I never knew. "All of this land," he swept a large hand over Nyverden, my country. "It's all in chaos."

"What about the queen? Isn't she keeping, you know, order?"

"The queen? Don't be naive. Her reign has long crumbled to pieces. Isn't witchcraft illegal in Nyverden?"

"Yes."

"Then how did a family of warlocks come to power in one of the most important ports in the country?"

I thought for a moment, but he didn't give me time to answer. "Nyverden has gone to ruin. It is within you power, Eli, to save your country."

"With a demon army? That just sounds like more chaos to me." Now I could see where this was going, and I didn't like it. All the fancy clothes and the fine food, it was all a bribe. He didn't rescue me for nothing, and it sounded like Aengel wasn't even supposed to be here. I walked right into the trap.

Wow, Eli.

"You're young," the large man said. "You wouldn't understand things like this."

"You're right, I don't understand." I wanted very much to be back in the forest now, safe in my little hut where no one could find me.

"My offer is this: you repay my hospitality with allowing me to counsel you on the movements of your army. I wouldn't want to see you use your power improperly."

I stepped back. "Who said I was ever going to raise an army?" I certainly had no intention to.

Why would I intentionally unleash evil?

That laugh boomed through the icy room. "Why wouldn't you?"

I told him demon armies weren't really my thing.

His face turned a hostile shade of red. "Don't be ridiculous, you cannot let this chance for peace pass you by. It's Nyverden's last chance for order!" His bloodshot eyes were starting to bulge in frustration. I my palms started to sweat. This guy was about my size but wider.

"Well, my decision is final. Thank you for your hospitality and for rescuing me and my friend from Mortis, but we really must be going." I had two more friends to find.

"You can't leave."

"What?" Sure I could. Here I go. Leaving.

"You may not leave until you start thinking clearly." He suddenly grabbed be by the arm and practically threw me out of the room, slamming the door behind him. I stood there for a moment, feeling utterly stupid for believing that this was all in genuine hospitality and not in a selfish desire for power. Believing the best in people has always been a vice of mine, but at least I'm not bitter about it.

I'm not.

Determined not to be anyone's prisoner again, let alone this guy who thought I was an ignorant baby, I stormed back to the hallway with Aengel and my's rooms. I banged on her door.

Silence.

I pounded my fists on the ice until chips flew off and showered me with their cold bites.

Nothing.

I threw open the door and scanned the room frantically.

No one.

I thought that may she had gone to my room for some reason and was waiting for me there. I thundered over and I only found an empty room.

She was gone.

"Aengel!" I called down the hallway. I started in the direction of the wooden door we found earlier. Losing all dignity by the time I turned the first corner, I sprinted down the icy halls, more than one stumbling and sliding on the impractical floor. I was roaring now. I knew now that this castle was no vacation and we were not guests here. We were prisoners. Over and over again, I screamed her name into the empty corridors. My desperate voice echoed back as my only answer.

Chapter 21

I was heaving in my oxygen by the time I finally reached the wooden door. Forcing it open, I found Aengel in the center of the room, alone.

"Stop, Eli!"

I paused mid-run, almost falling on my face. I looked around, seeing only the wooden walls and the girl in the center of them. I noticed that her once-perfect bun now had rebellious locks of hair on the loose and her dress, which was in pristine condition at lunch, was now rumpled and torn at the hem.

"What happened to you? Are you alright?" I stepped forward despite her pleas for me to stay back. "Did he hurt you?" I demanded.

"No, no. I'm fine, really! Please, Eli! Don't come any closer. You need to run!"

"Can you come to me then?"

"No." She was grimacing, like she was about to cry. "Please go."

"I can't just-"

The heavy door slammed shut like a crash of thunder.

A low laugh filled the room.

"Good, good. I'm glad you've found each other. This makes things so much more- interesting." I turned and saw Lord Yaroslavek strolling towards me with his hands clasped behind his back.

"*What have you done to her?*" I roared.

He smiled cruelly, staring at her like she was a little ant about to meet the bottom of his boot. "She's cursed."

I looked at her and saw her hope crumble. The eyes that once sparkled were now lifeless. A tear slid down her cheek.

"How?" I demanded.

"It's called a cupidon curse. I wasn't sure if it would work on you two, but last night confirmed my suspicions."

"What the hell is a cupidon curse?" I was yelling in his face now, being rude to my host didn't matter so much anymore.

"Tell him," the Lord said.

Aengel whimpered as if she had fallen from heaven and broken her wing in Hell. "It makes a girl be in pain when the man she loves is close. The closer he comes, the greater the pain." A single tear slipped down her perfect cheek.

"No," I whispered.

"It was a Warglien invention. Oh to be in love," Yaroslavek said. "What Mortis wouldn't give to know this."

I stood there like an idiot, utterly helpless to stop the world from crashing down on me. Love? Maybe partners in crime, or even a form of friendship, but love? Was that what is was? Was this the reason every time I looked at her my heart would feel like it was in my throat?

"Leave her out of this," was all I managed to choke out.

"And take away your motivation? Why would I do that, Eli my boy?" He wrapped his arm around my shoulder. "You and I, Eli, are going to change the world."

"And if I refuse?" I croaked.

"I chain you two together and see how long she lasts."

I couldn't speak. I couldn't breathe. There seemed to be something in my throat that just made it impossible. If I spoke, then the walls would crack and I'd come crashing down.

"I'll give you some time to think things over. I want my answer by dinner tonight." He looked back at us and smiled before disappearing behind the door. "You're both invited." The slam of the door behind him had a ring of finality in it.

It turned to her.

I wanted to be angry, I really did. I could deal with anger.

She was in pain and it was my fault.

A single tear slipped down my green cheek.

"I'm sorry," was all she said.

For a long, breathless moment I stood there. The air felt hollow- like someone had taken all the live-giving stuff out of it and left the emptiness.

Silence. I tried to stay strong.

"It's not your fault. I'm the sorry one."

She forced a painful laugh. "Do you know why I stole your stupid bracelet that first day we met?" I shook my head, not trusting myself to speak. "I never touched you, you know. I got the vision years ago from my mother. She passed on the vision to me when she met your parents. My *purpose* in life was to find you that day and keep you from dying. And that's been my purpose ever since. My mother knew you were the key to killing Mortis, and from the moment I was born, it was my mission to help you how ever I could. I always knew who you were, even before you told me about the dungeon at the Antimarx. My job was to help you, and I failed. I'm the one who should be sorry."

Her hands were shaking.

"We're going to make it out of this," I vowed, looking directly into those big green eyes. "I would hug you, because you look like you need one, but I don't want to kill you." She laughed, and wiped her face with her sleeve. "I have a plan, but first I have a question."

"What?"

"How do you break a cupidon curse?"

She shrugged, "Either I start hating you or we find a warlock who can lift it. I happen to know Czara can, so we just need to find her again."

"Yeah, I wonder where those guys ended up." This was such a casual conversation compared to how I was feeling.

"What was your plan?"

"If I hit it hard enough, I'm sure I can break the door, I just need to know that you can run on the ice and in the snow without me carrying you."

"I just need to know how you plan on breaking an oak door."

I smiled proudly. "I am a half orc, I'll have you know. And half elf." I sauntered over to the door and studied it for the moment. It looked pretty solid, definitely not cracked or worn in any way, shape, or form. I took a few steps away from it, trying not to get too close to Aengel, and then threw myself in the center of the wood.

Ow.

The world went white for a couple of seconds.

I held my face. "Did it work?"

"No."

I told her to get back so I could have a better running start. Before she could protest, I wound up and sprang.

I saw stars that time. They twinkled in the blank that filled my vision.

"-li! Eli!"

Someone was saying my name.

"Eli! Can you hear me?" I nodded delicately, as if there was a glass of water balancing on my head. "For the *love* of God, stop trying to *kill* yourself!"

Love. I like love. Why would I try and kill myself? Who does that? That's silly...

"I knew this was a bad idea. You and your brilliance," Aengel said from across the room. "You look awful, sit down and let me make the plans now." I complied and fiddled mindlessly with my bootlace. My head throbbed. Thoughts whizzed past me, and I couldn't seem to really hold on to one for longer than a second.

I heard this whooshing sound.

At first I thought it was the headache, or maybe an aspicien thing I didn't know about, or maybe the castle was making the noise. Suddenly, a little man, about as tall as my shin, materialized in front of me.

Great, now I'm hallucinating.

I must've hit my head harder than I thought.

The little man spoke, and I thought I'd reached a new level of crazy.

"We can help, sir."

I looked at my apparition and wondered whether I should respond or not.

"Sir? You don't look so good."

"Aengel!" I said. "I think I'm seeing things!"

She shook her head. "No, you're not. Who are you?" she said to the figment of my imagination.

"I'm Ada," the little mouth said. "I think the master calls us auxiliatrix, you usually don't see us."

Yeah, usually I don't hallucinate.

"How are we seeing you know?" I said. I narrowed my eyes at him, seeing if I could tell if he was real or not by taking in account every fiber of golden hair on his little head.

"Because I'm letting you, of course." he had a jolly little laugh. "The others and I have decided to help you get out of here."

"Out?" *Why would they help us?*

"Yes, silly," he smiled. He reminded me of a Christmas elf, to be honest. Like the kind my mother used to tell me about, reminding me that we were not *that* kind of elf because those don't exist. Well she was wrong. Clearly there was one standing right in front of me.

"How?" Aengel said. She was skeptical of Santa's little helper.

"We'll make you impossible to see! Then we can show you out. We won't leave it at that though, you'll need a sleigh."

"Thanks," God does answer prayers.

It hurt to stand up, but I ignored it, and followed the little guy out the door he somehow got open with the wave of his tiny hand. Aengel walked at a distance behind us, careful not to get too close. We made it out with little trouble, and there was a fully prepared sleigh waiting for us, horse already hitched and blankets loaded.

I stopped on the threshold of the back door we were sneaking out of. "How are we going to sit in there if we can't get close to each other?"

"I thought of that." He pulled a little vial out of his thin sleeve. "I stole this from the master. It should work for a couple hours, but that's all." I looked back into the hallway where she was waiting.

"Why are you helping us?" I said.

"Anything to screw the master."

Not such a jolly little man after all...

He scampered over to give Aengel the vial, and then disappeared. I said my thanks, even though I couldn't see him. Somehow I knew he was there.

I saw her take the vial and drink whatever was inside. We waited a couple minutes for the potion to kick in, just to be sure. After a couple minutes, we heard the alarms being raised that the prisoners were escaping. That was our cue to run to the sleigh.

"You good?" I grabbed the reigns.

"Yeah. Just get us out of here!"

I flicked the leather straps and commanded the horse to run.

Chapter 22

My head throbbed as the sleigh cut through the snow at incredible speed. Lunch rose in my throat. I forced myself to swallow it back down. The last thing we needed was for me to get sick all over our escape vehicle. Plus I'm not into recycling my food.

It was just before sunset, so I figured we had about fifteen to thirty minutes left of light. Lord Yaroslavek's dinner was probably getting cold. I hoped it would rot and then he'd eat it and suffer.

Not that I was bitter towards the guy, I just hated him.

We rode. The sound of pursuit was in the distance, and I wondered why they weren't getting any closer. Maybe little Ada had helped us out there too. The sun set, casting complete darkness over the barren landscape. The endless white became a depthless pitch. I think Aengel had fallen asleep because she had curled up in the blankets and her head rested carelessly on my arm. I prayed the potion would keep working until we found Czara and Luce. It was too dangerous for us to separate now. But then it would be too dangerous for us to stay together much longer.

Suddenly the sky lit up.

Beautiful lights beyond description filled the sky. There are no words for the moment when I first saw the celestial ribbon of color spiraling across the sky. I stopped the sleigh to marvel at their awesome beauty and decided that there had to be a God up there. There was no way that a world without a higher being would have lights like that in the sky that gave me this feeling that there's something greater up there that's far beyond me.

I remembered Aengel and woke her up just in time for us to see them fade back into the dark.

The darkness left us both breathless.

"Wow." It was all there was to say.

We sat there for a couple minutes, trying to wrap our heads around what we just saw. I've heard stories of the lights in the North, but I never thought they were real. I certainly never thought I, of all people, would ever see them.

The cold started to sink into our bones, and we silently agreed it was time to keep moving. Something had changed though. The moment when we saw the lights only got farther and farther away as the sleigh cut across the frozen land, but that feeling of awe didn't pass. Something had *changed*. I had no idea what that something was, exactly. She fell back asleep, and I forced the horse onward.

It was well into the night when the animal pulling the sleigh refused to pull it anymore. We had made it out of the boulder spotted plain into the snowy forest by then, the trees posing as our silent guardians from the eyes of the lord with the ice castle and the cellmate I once thought of as a friend. I sighed and relented, throwing one of the blankets on the ground for the horse to sleep on. He gave me a look of gratitude and curled up to rest. I nodded to the animal and whispered my own gratefulness for his part in our escape before wishing him a good night.

Luckily, my headache was feeling better. I probably gave myself some kind of concussion. Thanks to my elven blood, I heal at an incredible pace so I wasn't too worried. I had taken beatings worse than this from the kids back home and knew I'd be myself again in a day or two. The memory of why I left home in the first place came swelling up at me like an angry sea. I shoved it down before it could take root into my thoughts. I knew it was unorthodox, but it was cold and the sleigh was small. I huddled into my blankets next to Aengel, and fell asleep to the sound of her breathing.

✦✦✦✦

"Eli, wake up. Eli," someone was shaking my shoulder. I forced my eyes to open and saw bright green eyes lighting up my vision.

"Good morning," I mumbled as I pulled myself into sitting position. Suddenly I realized I had been flopped over on top of her, and the reason she woke me up was probably because it's not comfortable to be underneath 300 pounds of meat.

Real classy, Eli. Real classy...

I tried to laugh it off. "Sorry about that."

"You snore, you know." I saw her trying to hold back a smile.

"I do not!" I hopped out of the sleigh to hitch up the horse, thankful for the new winter boots I got back that the castle as part of the lord's bribery campaign. I patted his brown fur a couple of times, encouraging him to give us another good run today. We just needed to find a village before we froze to death or ran out of food. Ada had packed a sack of bread, dried fruit, and nuts I found under the seat. That would only last us about another day and a half though. The little guy was smart; He would've considered the distance to the closest towns while packing our food. I was sure of it.

After we hitched up, I got us moving in the same direction we had been going the night before. I couldn't help but feel like we were back that the beginning of our snow adventure. This time though, we had a horse and a sleigh. We didn't say much as we rode. I felt like we were walking on thin ice, waiting for that moment when we hear the sigh of the ice about to give out from under us. Any moment the potion could wear off and we'd be stranded in the middle of a frozen forest road with only one of us able to use the horse and sleigh and one of us will be screwed. Or, we'll both be screwed and stuck out here. I prayed that Yaroslavek wouldn't find us, and the potion would hold out until we found a village where we could get help. Heaven knows we needed it.

Aengel shifted uncomfortably, scooting as far away from me as the sleigh would allow. Sweat glistened on her forehead, despite the cold. She fingered her hair, twisting a strand of it around and around her index finger.

"You good?"

"Yes," she strained.

"You certainly look it. If it's too much. Please say something."

"I'm fine, Eli."

She grimaced and curled away from me. Her face was turned away, but I heard her choke on a sob.

"Whoa!" The horse slowed to a stop, but I was out of the sleigh before then. With each step I took back, the color returned to her face and I could see the pain drain away.

"I'll be back!" I called.

"Where are you going? Eli! You can't just *leave* me here!"

"I'll be back!" I repeated over my shoulder. If one can truly run in snow up to their mid-shin, I was running. I wasn't sure where I was going, exactly, or what I was looking for. All I knew was that I needed to put some distance between me and her and find someone or something to help us. I ran wildly and prayed like mad.

We needed help.

There was no way I could fix this on my own, and I knew that to the very core of my being. I ran and I ran and I ran. There was no direction except away. I was left exhausted and empty in every sense of the word. I was in the middle of the forest in deep winter with no supplies, no way to get close to my only traveling companion and friend, and no idea where I was going. I sank to my knees and allowed the soft snow to pull me down into its icy embrace. I let the cold seep through my skin and into my bones. With every passing moment, I sank deeper and deeper into the numbness.

How does one break a curse with no magic?

"Eli?"

I looked up.

"Eli? Are you okay?" I knew that boy. Heaving myself out of the snow and out of my helplessness, the ex-priest stood there, just happy to see me alive. I wasn't alone anymore.

"Luce, you have no idea how glad I am to see you." I did hug him then. He patted me awkwardly on the back until I released my overjoyed grapple. I didn't care, my dignity was long gone already.

"What were you doing in the snow like that?"

"I need your help."

He nodded, confused. "Sure, sure, anything."

"Where's Czara?" I scanned the woods around us. "How'd you guys get here?"

"It's a long story. Czara's with Aengel. We found her where you *left* her, she told us you ran off this way."

"I shouldn't have left her." That was bad of me.

"Whatever you say, boss." He led me back to the girls, and for a rare moment I was actually happy to see the half elf.

"Well if it isn't the orc," she released a rare smile.

"I missed you too, Czara."

"Where did you go?" Aengel poked her head out from behind her.

"I was looking for this kind of bark, it would've helped with the pain." The priest with medical training and the experienced apothecary looked at me. They knew I was a trained healer. They also knew there would be no kind of bark in these woods to have anything to do with pain. And anyways, it would need to be made into a tea or something, and we had no way to do that out here. But Aengel didn't know that. I put my good faith in Czara that she wouldn't question it, and in Luce that he wouldn't either.

So I lied. Kill me.

"Well," the half elf said. "There's no need for it now. I stripped her spells off."

"What do you mean 'spells'? She only had one curse."

"Oh please orc, it's not unheard of for a girl like her to have a couple charms here and there. We live in the city all our lives, a little protection isn't such a bad idea."

Aengel nodded. "I had a charm against some sicknesses, but I guess I'll just have to wash up more now."

"How'd you get a charm?" I said.

"My mother asked an elven healer or something, I don't know," Aengel said. "People get them all the time, like tattoos."

"You have a tattoo?"

Her face reddened. "Of course not."

Czara smiled. "I do." I didn't ask to see it. Some things are better left a mystery.

"Well," I said. "We should probably keep moving. Do you guys know if there's a town nearby?"

"Yeah," Luce pointed south, which was straight ahead for us on the path. "About five miles down that way."

"Good, let's load up and head there." It was a tight squeeze, but we all managed to fit in the sleigh. Luce was openly grateful for not having to walk in the snow, but if Czara was grateful, she didn't show it.

I wanted to ask how they found us, or how they even managed to get away from Mortis, but didn't. For one moment in time, I wanted to pretend that I wasn't capable of bringing on the end of the world and that we were just four friends out for a sleigh ride. I wanted to pretend that I wasn't on the run from three different, and powerful, people. Then maybe, just maybe, I'd forget that I don't live back with the Tribe anymore and that the place I called home was now abandoned. I could pretend that my mother was still alive and that I had never known about warlocks, aspiciens, demons, priests or prophecies.

See, that's what happens when you have too much time to think.

Chapter 23

We made it to a little outpost town by lunch time. It certainly wasn't nearly as big as Shatterpoole, but that's probably because it's the largest port in Nyverden. The streets were packed dirt, but there was a main street of shops and an inn. Cozy but not overstated, the inn was a welcomed rest stop after a long night in the cold. I told myself I'd never sleep out in a sleigh again if I could help it. The same room protocol was used in this inn as we had used before. There was a boy's bedroom, and the girl's one was next to it.

"Although I'm sure you and Aengel wouldn't mind sharing," I heard Czara snicker.

"So what did you and Luce do these past few days? Sleep an arm's length apart? Make sure you'd never go within six inches of each other?"

She narrowed her icy eyes at me and popped up the collar on her black leather jacket. I watched her sulk off, probably towards the bar. I went into the room I was sharing with the ex-priest and rolled on my claimed bed. It had a quilt and a wool blanket in consideration of the weather, making it very comfy to lie on top of. I took in that peaceful moment. It wasn't too often now that I could just close my eyes and let the world be without me for a couple of minutes.

"Hey boss," I heard Luce come in and sink on to the bed on the opposite side of the small room.

"Hey," I didn't bother to open my eyes.

"Did you hear what they've been saying downstairs?"

I opened one eye. "No."

"Apparently the queen's had an affair. People are saying that she killed the king on purpose."

"What?" I sat up. The king had died almost a year ago from some mysterious illness. People get sick all the time, it's not like there were too many health codes around here. I'd never heard of anyone blaming the queen for it though.

"Why? Why now?"

Luce shrugged. "She had a baby with red hair, people talk, she's doing an awful job running the country, I don't know."

"What does her baby's hair color have to do with it?"

"Well, all her other kids have black or brown."

"Do you realize how ridiculous that sounds?"

He threw his hands up. "That's just what people have been saying. I think it's also worth mentioning that the baby would had to have been conceived the week he died or a little after.

"And yet people are pointing out the kid's hair color first?"

"I think it's concerning they're pointing anything out at all," Luce said.

"Yeah, I know I didn't get out much before Shatterpoole, but I always remembered people liking the queen."

Luce's eyes had a hint of blue sorrow in them. "She used to be a great ruler, now she's just an angry woman on a throne with too many kids and too much power."

"Isn't that treason?" I raised an eyebrow.

"Yup."

I flopped back down on my bed. *What is this country coming to?* No, what is this world coming to. People just don't go around talking about their queen like that. She used to be really popular among the lower class, actually. Queen BaBelle was a peasant girl who married the long-lost bastard prince who happened to be the last in line for the throne when the previous royal family died off from the tuberculosis plague. They tracked him down through orphanage records, and in a night he went from being a nameless lumber worker named Job to king of the biggest kingdom in the known world, and she went with him. They were both about 19 at the time and had their first son already. The whole thing was shocking to the people, and the story of underdogs becoming royals caused fanfare all over the kingdom. Ten years later, the people were less excited about having BaBelle on the throne, I guess. Personally, I never really had a problem with her. There was little need for politics out in the woods.

Our door burst open. Czara charged in before I could scramble out of bed.

"We need to go. *Now*."

I hurried to pull on my boots. Silently I wished that I had grabbed one of the coats from the trunk of clothes Yaroslavek had tried to bribe me with.

"What is it?" I said. Luce was pulling together his back pack, brow fixed. It was curious to me how he had managed to get his back from the Mortis's house. They had taken our stuff when the guards escorted us in. Now the only things I had left from my life before this adventure were the scars and my father's bracelet.

"An angry Santa Claus is asking around town for you and Aengel. And you don't blend in." Well, at least I know the drunks talk about something productive down there.

"Thanks." I pushed past her and found Aengel waiting in the hallway. She still had on that ripped white dress. She didn't blend in either. I motioned to her to follow me down the stairs, the other two followed behind. *Next town we go to, we'll have to get new clothes,* I decided, a*nd backpacks.*

The four of us hurried down through the back door and into the stables. I realized I'd have to forget my morals this time if I wanted us to get away.

"Forget the sleigh, everyone grab a horse, we need to move quickly." Aengel and Luce looked surprised, but

Czara just smiled. I think she took pleasure in watching me break my own rules.

I grabbed the horse that Ada gave us with the sleigh. He bobbed his brown head up and down, excited to finally get to go out again. If I didn't know any better, I'd say this guy actually liked running for his life. I wished we could've traded places.

"Let's go!" I said. We didn't have the cover of night- it was late afternoon at best. And I was hungry. I tried not to fall off the horse and led my team back into the woods as fast as I could. Luce shouted directions at me until I let him go in front of me to lead. I'm directionally challenged. It's an issue. I also stink at horseback riding, and having the horse running didn't make it any easier. At least my headache was gone.

And I hate to say this, but thanks to Czara's drinking problem and sharp ears, we made it out safe and sound without Yaroslavek ever seeing us. After a while of making the horses run through the sparse winter woods, we slowed them to a walk so we could all catch our breath and dig into the nuts and bread Luce had gotten from the inn back in town and what we had left from Ada. I pulled my horse up next to Aengel up on her gray mare.

"How are you doing?"

"I'm fine," she said, pulling at a strand of red hair.

"You cold?" All she had on was that dress, which was long sleeved, but still not fit for walking around in the snow. I was wearing a waistcoat for my second layer, so it's not like I was better off.

"I'll live," she smiled.

I unbuttoned that stupid waistcoat and shrugged it off. "Here, take it. You'll freeze to death." We had no coats, and left the blankets in the sleigh.

"And you won't?"

I shook my head and she reluctantly picked it out of my hand. It wasn't much, but it was better than a ripped dinner party dress. I noticed Czara looking at me with a satisfied smirk on her ruby red lips. Luce was playing it cool and acting like he hadn't see anything.

"Okay, let's head out." Everyone groaned. Luce took his place as navigator with me not far behind. The girls trailed, Czara as the caboose. Trying not to be too obvious, as I scanned the forest to look for some place to set up camp, I'd catch glimpses of red hair and green eyes. Our eyes caught for a brief, terrified second before I snapped my head back around. I decided not to risk it again and kept her out of my line of vision.

I saw a shack to our right a little ways off the path and suggested we go check it out. If there was people there we could ask for supplies and shelter, if not, we'd be squatters for a night. The closer we rode to the cabin, the more I was leaning towards the squatter deal. It was old in the worst way. The wood was gray and rotten, and the windows were too dirty to see through. One was broken. I slipped off my horse and walked up to the weathered door, barely hanging onto its rusted hinges. Out of some sort of memory of custom, I knocked on the splintered wood.

"Eli! What are you knocking for? No-"

Czara closed her mouth as the door silently eased open. I stepped back.

"Hello?" I could feel my pulse pounding in my throat. I looked into the dark.

And the darkness looked back.

"Come in," it croaked.

I looked back at my group standing at the edge of the trees with the horses. Their expressions ranged from curious to terrified.

"Who are you?" I tried to see through the space between the door and the rotten frame without getting too close.

"We are the Eyes That See Through Time."

How the heck am I supposed to respond to that?

"Um, sorry to bother you," I backed up, changing my mind about asking whoever was in the shack for help. "We'll just be on our way now."

"No, no," the darkness said. "Come in, we've been waiting for you, Eli son of Fair and Foul."

"How do you know me?" Since when did I have a kick-butt nickname?

A low chuckle leaked from behind the wood.

"We know everything." The door eased open to widen the yawning crack, revealing three stooped women, as old as time itself, dressed in ragged black cloth held together with dead leaves. Their skin was so sunken and sallow that they looked more like corpses than old women. The one in the center of their huddle wagged a bony finger at me.

"Come in," she croaked.

Aengel, Luce, and Czara were beside me in an instant.

"He's not going anywhere," Czara said.

Aengel nodded. "Anything you have to say to him you can say out here."

The three of them laughed as if they were one person. Icy chills ran down my spine, leaving a knot in my empty stomach.

"Son of the Fair seeks something," the first hag said.

"Son of the Foul seeks a weapon," said the second.

The third one gave another chilling laugh. "The boy seeks to kill a demon."

I didn't waste anyone's time asking how they knew. It seemed that the world was a more mysterious place than I had ever imagined when I left home.

"What do you want from me?" seemed like a much more appropriate question.

"A single drop of blood to pay our price."

"Price for what?"

Ink

"Where the animula is."

I looked at Aengel, then Luce, then Czara. We needed this. I'm sure that eventually we'd find our way to the only thing that could kill Mortis, but this was a free handout. It would have been mad to pass this up. Besides, what was a drop of blood anyways?

"Okay." I lifted my hand towards them. The one with the bracelet that started this whole shenanigans.

"Eli! You can't give them your blood! They're witches, who knows what they'll do with it!" Aengel yanked my outstretched hand away from them.

"What are we supposed to do? Pass this up?"

She was insistent. "When they ask for blood, yes."

Czara sighed. "Luce isn't going to find it any time soon in those ridiculous books of his, and we're running out of time before Mortis or Yaroslavek or someone stops us. If you haven't noticed, we're being hunted here. If we have a chance to one-up everyone, I say we take it."

"Czara's right," Luce admitted. "The trail ends here for the animula. There are no more clues."

"I'm sorry, Aengel." I gave the center hag my massive hand. The moment her clammy hand clutched mine, frozen waves shot through my entire body. My knees shook, and I was unsure that my feet would keep me stable. She slid a jagged dagger out of her clothes and hovered the uneven blade above my hand.

I agreed to give a drop *of blood, not my entire freaking hand!*

"Hey! I-"

She sliced the blade over my palm and red, angry liquid oozed from the path it had made over my skin.

"I don't-"

She tipped my hand, letting the blood drip into a little glass vial one of her sisters had waiting. I watched as my life drained out of me into that little glass. When it was filled, she thrust my hand back to me. I gave a small whine as I pressed the bloody wound on the white button up I got from my time in the ice castle. Stinging and still dripping blood, I curled around my hand to try and find some sort of relief.

"Now tell us where the animula is," I demanded, lifting my eyes.

"The birthplace of Missi Mortis."

The door slammed shut, and all life inside seemed to vanish.

"I'll wrapped that up for you," Luce offered. I was grateful that there was another healer besides myself here. He pulled the healing kit that Sal had given us when we left the Blue Bear, and started to treat my hand. It must've been in his pack when he got it back from Mortis. Sal. The Bear. It seemed like a lifetime ago.

Night was coming on, and we needed to find a place to camp. We were all hungry and tired, and had a big traveling day tomorrow. Uninterested in sleeping near the three old crones who sliced my hand, we went about a half a mile away before finding a clearing and setting up there. We didn't bother to set up both of the tents we had left, just one for the girls. I was fine sleeping on the frozen ground as long as I had a blanket under me. I took the rough one from under my horse's saddle, and curled up next to him while Czara made a fire. Aengel was out somewhere changing into Czara's extra clothes so she didn't have to wear the ripped dress, and Luce was studying his notes to figure out where Mortis was born. I was almost asleep when Aengel came back. She was clad head to toe in black leather. I'm sure she was warmer, but I'm also sure that she was slightly uncomfortable. If I knew anything, she was adamant about girls wearing dresses and leaving the pants wearing to the boys. She looked like a real adventurer now, her big black boots crunching on the frozen leaves. The only thing characteristic of her appearance was her playful red waves of hair.

"You're staring," she said.

"No I wasn't." So maybe I was.

She gave me a look and joined Czara by the fire.

Cupidon curse my foot, there's no way even in the seventh circle of Hell that she even likes me.

My horse let out a nicker, and pushed his nose into my back.

"What? You hate me too?" He rested his heavy head on top of me. "I know you love me, you big mutt." I reached around and patted his nose. I always liked horses.

Chapter 24

Someone was nudging me in my back. I rolled over, shivering at the sudden cold I had kept off by curling up. Big brown horse eyes were staring at me.

"Good morning," I patted his head and pulled myself up to stand and stretch out from my night on the ground. I decided I would call him Nudger, since he always seemed to me sticking his nose into me. He needed a name anyways.

Luce was still sprawled out on the ground with his blanket, his and Czara's horses tied up not far away. Czara was already up and tending the fire, Aengel next to her trying to prepare a rabbit I'm assuming the half elf got us for breakfast. I checked around for Aengel's horse, just to make sure it hadn't run off, and saw it not far away and tied safely to a low branch. One thing was clear, Aengel had no idea had to gut an animal.

I walked over and kneeled beside her. "What are you doing to that poor thing?"

"Sal always handled the meat," she admitted.

"Here, let me do that," I lifted the little carcass away from her before she could mutilate it further. It was already dead for heaven sake.

"Don't worry, I've done this about a million times," I assured her. "My mother never really liked seeing an animal dead like this. I think that's why she never ate meat."

"Why do you then?" Aengel said.

I shrugged. "I respect the animal's death. It had to die sometime, this is the best way to go for a rabbit."

Czara snickered. "It's an animal and therefore food, you make it sound more poetic than it is, orc."

"Are you the only elf who eats meat?"

"I'm half demon, you're lucky I'm not eating you."
Aengel couldn't help but giggle at such a ridiculous
thought, but I didn't. I knew she wasn't joking.

Breakfast was ready by the time Luce woke up.
Snowflakes were started to sprinkle the ground while we
ate. We packed up before it really started coming down and
were on our way in the flurry. Luce said he knew where we
were headed, so we followed him down the forest path.

"It's not far from here!" he called back at us
through the snow.

"Well how far is it?" I said.

"We'll be there before sunset."

Whenever he says that, something bad always
happens after sunset, a werewolf town, for example.

We stopped to rest once the snow slowed down
around mid-morning. I took the folded blanket out from
under Nudger's saddle and used Luce's sword to cut a hole
for my head. Instant poncho. My bloody button up just
wasn't doing much against the cold. Aengel had returned
my waist coat since she had a leather jacket now, but I felt
weird wearing such a fancy piece of clothing out here in the
woods. Besides, my poncho was warmer. .

I called a lunch break around noon even though the
snow was picking up again. I figured it must've been about
late November by now. While we were finishing up the
rabbit from breakfast, I asked Luce and Czara how they got
away from Mortis.

"I'm a warlock, orc. I can get away from someone if
I want to."

"Yeah, but how?"

"It's called a 'relocation spell', I can only cast it
once a week because it gets too draining. I just had to find
Luce and cast it to where ever you guys were."

"You can teleport?" I shouldn't have been
surprised.

Before Czara could gloat about how she can do all kinds of things because she's, oh yes indeed, a warlock, Aengel said, "What happened once you got through the doors?"

Luce paled. Czara looked away for a terrible moment.

"I got us out," was all she said. I saw her close her eyes and relive the memory her mind seemed to dread.

I rushed through the door to escape the swirling gas pouring through the room. As soon as I entered, I was filled with the sour acid of regret and my stomach flipped to greet my throat.

I was in my old room.

Not the one at the orphanage, no. This was the room I slept in for only four years of my life. When I was a young girl of 13, though I looked sufficiently like a five year old human, Rhone came to collect me from the government orphanage. She was glamorously pregnant and so beautiful. I called her mother then.

The room I was standing in was in the town house Rhone bought to have her third child and raise me in. Supposedly. It was tucked in the one of the middle rings, where it was safe for children to play outside in the day and most of our neighbors had nannies and housekeepers. I knew Dragos was far up North with our father. He was too precious to live in such a mundane place as Shatterpoole. My bed was made up with a plush mattress and a black and red quilt with rose patterns. A crib was on the other wall, decorated with black tulle and green ribbons. I strode over to it thoughtfully and remembered looking at my baby sister, Syla, sleeping peacefully under the green and black blankets. I couldn't help but miss her then, I hadn't seen her in years.

There was a flickering darkness that descended on the room. I noticed then there were no windows. My heart began to throb against my rib cage. The door was gone. I was alone in my nursery with the darkness. The last bit of golden light blew out from some unseen candle.

It was dark.

I shut my eyes and clenched my fists so hard my nails began to cut the flesh of my palms.

Baby Czara's afraid of the dark.

I couldn't help but gasp. There was no one in the room. I knew it. My low light vision confirmed it as I scanned the last remaining shadows. But I heard my mother whisper clearly.

How did my little demon come to fear the dark? She snickered. You are the darkness.

"No, I'm not." I whispered back. My breath became ragged and the darkness turned into a black velvet cloth twisting around my face, suffocating me. A sob rose in my throat. I knew it was just a little lack of light. Darkness doesn't choke people. No. It's what's in the darkness.

Here's a lullaby to shut your eyes
It was always this that I despised
I don't feel enough for you to cry
Here's a lullaby to shut your eyes
Goodnight
Here's a lullaby to shut your eyes
It wouldn't be hard for me to lie
It was always this that I despised
Here's a lullaby to shut your eyes
Good night
Here's a lullaby to shut your eyes
It was always him that I despised
Waiting for poison's soft demise
There won't be one day you are mine
Goodbye

Sick. Sick. Sick. I wretched all over the worn carpet. The lullaby played over and over again in my mind as I sank to the floor to my knees.

"STOP IT!" I screamed at Mortis, at Rhone, at whoever the hell was playing my freaking sick lullaby over in my mind. I pulled at my hair and clawed at my face as if the pain could distract me, or maybe I could claw the pain rooted in my soul away with my long black fingernails. The velvet was choking me. I clawed at the floor and screamed. My nails didn't make contact with a carpet though. It was a gritty stone floor.

I scrambled over to a wall, swatting the air violently to find a solid thing in a liquid black darkness.

Here's a lullaby to shut your eyes

My eyes were clenched shut so they wouldn't have to face the infinite ebony. I found a stoney wall and then some rusty bars. I was in a dungeon. Hot, horrified tears streamed down my face.

I screamed again.

I shook my head.

There must've been something stuck in my ear, or eyes, or something.

I looked around and wondered where that awful vision came from, it certainly wasn't one of my memories. Czara's eyes locked with mine.

No, orc. It was mine.

What? Are you seriously talking to me with your mind right now?

Yes, don't act so surprised, I'm a-

A warlock, yeah, got that. Now get out of my head.

You know she likes you too, I knew she was talking about Aengel.

We have a mission.

You're no fun.

I ignored her snide remarks about me and Aengel until she gave up and got out of my head. I found myself still shuddering from her memory. The doors must've lead to that person's worst fear. That's what it looked like anyways. Thank goodness Aengel and I ended up at with Lord Yaroslavek. I didn't want to know what was behind the door for me. I didn't have the heart to ask Luce.

"Luce, where exactly are we going?"

"It's an abandoned monastery," he called back. "It's more like a pile of rocks now though."

While we rode to the monastery, the snow had tapered off and then altogether ceased. I tried to use the travel time wisely and think of ways to improve my leadership skills. Who knows why I got so self-conscious about them all of the sudden, maybe it was the way Aengel would look at me or the way Czara would snicker more often.

I never thought we'd finally get there, but I started seeing out of place boulders that looked like they were once used for a building. Maybe a building like a monastery in the middle of the forest on the border of Franken and Nyverden? I hoped so, because I wasn't sure how much longer I could last on a horse.

"We're here."

Perhaps Luce said we were "here", but all I saw was woods with a bunch of building stones scattered around.

"So," Czara said. "Where's the monastery?"

"Right here," he splayed his arms out. "We're here."

Aengel looked around some more. "I don't see anything."

Luce let out an exasperated sigh, but didn't say anything.

"Maybe," I said. "He was using the word 'abandoned' lightly when he said 'abandoned monastery'".

"Well this is what the map said, I can't help it if the place looks like crap."

"It doesn't even look like anything, priest."

Oh Czara, always one for the obvious.

I got off the horse, at least to stretch my legs if anything. Czara and Luce started arguing about something while Aengel kept them from killing each other. I stood there watching them and wondered when would be a good time to step in. They seemed like they needed to let off some steam anyways. Czara hadn't had anything except water all day. Something caught my eye and I looked down at the snow covered ground.

It was a knob.

Just sticking up out of the layer of snow was a simple metal knob. I would've easily missed it if the snow had been just a bit higher or I was less lucky/observant/who-*really*-knows. I bent down to pick it up and, not to my surprise, it wouldn't budge. Not about to give up so easily, I started clearing out all the snow around it. My hands were cold, but that was survivable.

"What are you doing?" I picked up my head for a second to see Aengel walk over to me. Apparently the fight had finished and I saw Luce glaring at the half elf with a new level of dislike next to one of the horses. It would pass. It always did. I had a feeling that he had something for her.

"I'm digging. There's a knob here in the ground."

"What?" she kneeled down in the snow with me and we uncovered an iron door. Luce and Czara had joined the efforts by the time we found the edges and found the whole thing. It might've been a close fit for a guy like me, but I could make it. We all took in a deep breath and I twisted and pulled. It came open this time, revealing stone stairs that disappeared into darkness after the first couple steps.

I looked into the black. "Who wants to go first?"

Nobody said anything, so I shrugged and started feet first down the hole in the ground. It wasn't a monastery, but it was something. The steps were short, steep, and narrow. Concentrating not to slip and fall down into the dark, I ignored all these nagging feelings that told me that maybe I *shouldn't* be climbing down these mysterious stairs into the alleged birthplace of a greater demon and my current worst enemy. Well I didn't expect him to have been born in a normal place like a normal person.

The light of the fading day disappeared now. That didn't bother me because I can see in the dark, but Aengel and Luce were struggling above me. Luce was the last one in and he couldn't stop looking up at the now-distant light. The two of us that had backpacks were having more trouble than Aengel and me. I would've taken Luce's or Czara's if either of them weren't so proud. I'm clearly more suited to carrying heavy things than the ex-priest or the little half elf.

How long are these stairs?

A scream.

I see Czara tumbling towards me with the two humans on top of her. We all fly through the darkness like a butterball of man, orc, and elf. A screaming butterball. I might've mentioned more than once how I was going to kill that blind priest, but it was hard to hear over the sounds of our combined screams.

Chapter 25

I hurt all over. Thankfully I managed not to hit my head too hard, and judging from the moans around me, nobody was dead. They can thank me for being a meat cushion. I made a roll call and everyone was okay, more or less. Luce was sorry. That didn't make anyone less annoyed at him for making us all fall down about a hundred stairs.

Once everyone was present and accounted for, I looked around. It was just a tunnel carved out of packed dirt, leading into stone walls and a stone floor. There were dormant torches lining the walls, but other than that, it was just us and the tunnel.

"Well," I said. "I guess the only way to go is forward."

"What about the horses?" Aengel rubbed her forearm, trying to relieve some of the pain. By the way she was moving it and how things looked, I'd say it was sprained.

"They'll be fine," I helped her off the ground. "We shouldn't be too long and they won't run off far." *I hope.*

Czara saw right through my bullcrap. Luce too, but he was too busy picking up the scattered contents of his pack to give me any looks. Aengel trusted me too much.

I helped Luce organize the healing kit that burst open when he had hit the ground, and organize the rest of his things. Czara led the way, lighting the torches with her purple fire as we went along. She and I could've done without them, but the humans needed the light. I followed close behind and kept my eyes peeled for anything that might be dangerous up ahead. Nobody spoke. It may have only looked like a tunnel, but the place had this certain feel around it. It was like walking through a graveyard at dusk-you don't see anything dangerous, but the very air makes your nervous. Subconsciously, I forced my feet not to make a sound. I didn't want to wake the souls of graves I was walking on.

It was unsettling.

I stopped short once because a rat scuttled over my foot, and Aengel slammed into me. I hadn't noticed her right on my heels.

We quickly regained our balance and kept moving, ignoring the fact we were all huddling abnormally close together. It felt more dangerous to stop than to keep going into the tunnel. One would think it'd be the other way around. I guess I just felt more vulnerable standing still. For the first half hour, the tunnel seemed to go on and on forever. I tried not to worry about the horses back up top and just kept moving. All there seemed to be down here was tunnel. More tunnel. And, yes, more tunnel.

Something moved up ahead.

I threw a hand up, "hold on, guys."

Everyone stopped and looked at me curiously. And anxiously. It was where Missi Mortis was created, it would've been foolish *not* to be concerned. After a few seconds of staring hard into the dark, I decided nothing was there. I was just being paranoid.

"Never mind, I mus-"

The tunnel filled with this *horrible* squeaking noise, drowning me out. Suddenly we heard a thousand rats skitter over the stone floor. It didn't take long before I realized the wretched sound was getting louder, and louder, and louder.

And louder.

I freaking hate rats.

They were swarming towards us like a vermin-tsunami. Someone screamed and we all ran. Our way was already lit by the torches. Luce was ahead, I was less fast on my feet and Aengel and less so. Czara was behind us spraying flames from her hands thrust behind her as she ran down the tunnel.

"Burn, bitches! Burn!"

For a moment there, it seemed like she was actually having fun- the time of her life actually. It was cut short though, when we hit a stone wall.

Yes. A wall.

Wasn't this supposed to be a tunnel?! How the Hell does this happen?

Luce was the first to hit it, slamming his fists into it like that would do anything.

The rats forced our backs against the cold stone, squeaking like little rodent-demons. Czara kept them back with her fire, but for every hundred that burned, 200 took their place. A gruesome pile of carcasses collected in front of us like a mass grave.

"Go away!" Aengel screamed. They swarmed all the more closer.

My hands were sweating and I just couldn't control my breathing. Looking over to my left, I thought I saw Luce praying. His head was bowed, golden hair dipping down under gravity, lips moving quickly but silently. I was about to look away out of respect for his newfound religion that I could never have, before I was blinded.

Brilliant, white light shot out of every pale inch of skin on his body. My eyes stung from the sudden, searing light even after I threw my hands over them. The flash only lasted for a few seconds before disappearing back into the priest. It took a minute for my eyes to adjust back to the dimness, but when they did, the rats were gone. Except for the dead ones, courtesy of Czara. They were too dead to run away from Luce's celestial light.

"What the Hell was that?" Aengel said. Czara and I were still blinking like crazy to get those annoying spots out of our vision. Seeing in the dark does have its cons- like extra light sensitivity and only having yourself to blame when you trip over stuff at night.

Luce smiled, "I had no idea I could do that."

"Well neither did I," I said, rubbing my eyes.

"What did you do?" Aengel said. Czara just looked at him. Long and hard.

"It was a light spell I found a year ago when I was reading *The Effects of Light on Dark Creatures*. Terrible book, but some interesting stuff."

"I thought Priests of Darkness only studied darkness," Czara said.

"The book was in the restricted section, I only got it because the guy who supplies our books in the monastery has a desperate daughter."

I raised an eyebrow.

"I said I never wanted to be a priest."

There was so little I knew about Luce, that I felt like I had to ask, but now was not the time for stories.

"I don't doubt you, man." I said. "But good thing you were a priest or we'd never be able to find this place."

"And get trapped in a demon-rat infested Hell-hole? You're welcome," he looked away.

Aengel shook her red head. "We're not trapped, we're just not going the right way."

"It's a tunnel, sunshine," Czara flicked back her hair. "There's only two ways to go. That way" she pointed down the hall. "And this way," she jabbed a finger at the wall.

"Not if this isn't a tunnel," Luce said.

I was confused, I guess. "But this wall clearly wasn't here before."

"No," he turned to me. "I think this might be a Shifting Maze."

We all looked at him.

He smiled, despite everything. "You guys have never heard of these before? That's forgivable, they're fairly ancient. It's exactly what it sounds like: a maze that shifts around to make it almost impossible to get out."

"So we're trapped?" I folded my arms.

"I said '*almost* impossible'."

"I'm listening."

"The weakness of the maze is- well, nobody knows."

Czara let out an irritated snort. "Then why did you just say that? Are you trying to make us miserable?"

"No!" he protested. "The wizard who made the mazes said there was a weakness to their design but died before telling anyone."

"How'd he die?" Aengel asked.

"Demon."

I guess that pretty much summed it up.

"Does anyone know the weakness?" I asked.

"Nobody survives the mazes. I should've known this 'monastery' was one."

"No," Aengel pushed back her orange hair. "I'm the prophetess, I should've known."

Czara and I shook our heads. It went without saying that this was really nobody's fault. We all thought it was a monastery.

"Since we can't just stand here and feel bad about it, I say we keep walking. Maybe we'll figure out how to beat this thing, maybe we'll find a door, if we're lucky, we might even find the animula- who knows," I started down the hallway where the rats had come from with nowhere else to go. One by one, Aengel, Luce, and finally Czara trailed behind me. My feet were moving, but my mind was racing on a different track. I didn't even see the ancient tunnel surrounding me. My entire concentration capacity was honed on the weakness of the walls. I was, by no means, a magic-expert, but I wasn't unintelligent. Czara might've disagreed with that, but opinions are opinions. Scraping my mind for anything useful on this, I only came out with frustration and a headache. My concentration broke when we hit a dead end and had to turn left into another tunnel.

"Did this change or had we not been here before?" I heard Aengel say behind me.

I wasn't sure, and there was no way I could be, but I just told her this was new territory. We had been walking for long enough.

Czara had taken up the front again, lighting the torches, and Luce took the back, deep in thought. I took a break from thinking about the maze and just tried to notice the things around me. I could hear Aengel's delicate footsteps behind me, smell the dampness of being underground, and hear the occasional dreaded scampering of- yuck- rats.

My stomach growled.

"I'm hungry," there was no point trying to get out of here if I was just going to starve myself. Our caravan halted, startled almost by my bluntness. After calling for the rest, I turned to talk to Luce, knowing he had walnuts in his backpack.

"Come up with anything good yet?" I shoved a few nuts in my mouth and washed them down with some water from his canteen. Thank goodness he filled it when we were up top. Thank goodness he's a good sharer.

"No, not really. Nobody really knows anything about Shifting Mazes. I have a couple theories, but nothing logical."

"Wanna know what I think?" I jumped a little. I didn't even noticed Czara standing next to me.

"Sure," he looked at her, devoting full attention.

"I think Mortis is screwing with our heads again and this is all a simulation."

Aengel slid over in between me and the half elf and gave a gentle smile, "you read too many political pamphlets, Czara."

I thought for a moment. Maybe there was something to what she was saying. Not the sarcasm, but the simulation idea. Magic's mechanics remained a mystery to me, but it would make sense that good magic is solid. If you turned a grape into a gold coin and the magic was solid, it would stay a gold coin. All we knew about Shifting Mazes were that they *shifted.*

Wouldn't that make it unstable? And if the spell is unstable because of how inconstant it is, is their solidity just an illusion?

I shared this with the other three, and they each thought about it for a good second.

"That actually makes sense," Luce said at last. "How do we apply that though?"

"More like, how does a half orc come up with that?"

"I'm a half elf too, Czara," I shot back. I was sure to turn away before she gave me a signature smirk. "We should keep moving." Our packs were back together in no time, and we were on our way again into the shifting dark.

Chapter 26

There's something about stone that makes it almost impossible to sleep on. Maybe because it sucks the heat right out of you, or maybe it's because every knob and jut in your body bruises on the rock. When I called for us to break camp in the middle of the tunnel, I had sleep in mind- not lying awake and feeling every crack in the stone floor. I shifted, trying to figure out a comfortable spot. The others were asleep around me, the girls a little farther away from Luce and me out of custom. Luce's soft snores filled the tunnel, and I heard Aengel mutter something about strawberries.

Then something else.

Squeak, squeak, squeeeak.

I sat up and scanned the darkness. There was nothing out there except for me and my friends. Hesitantly, I laid back down and tried to shut my eyes.

Squeak, squeak-

I shot up and threw the horse blanket off of me so I could stand. Nothing was there, but I couldn't trust my eyes. I walked around our little 'camp' for a minute, making sure we didn't have any unwanted visitors. Nothing. Then I heard the squeaking again a little ways down the tunnel.

"Hello?"

I don't know why I thought anything hiding in the dark would actually answer me.

Finally I caught a glimpse of a shadow scampering on the wall. Exhausted but curious, I chased after the little bugger. He led me down and down the tunnel and then through a left turn. I prayed the maze wouldn't change and I'd be able to find my way back. Only his shadow was visible to me, I never actually saw the rat I thought I was following. Farther and farther away I went, going faster and faster to try and catch him. Then I hit a dead end, the wall finalizing my search. Still no rat; He wasn't there. I looked around the wall and back tracked a little before deciding to give up.

"Sofiel?"

I stopped dead and slowly turned around. A young woman was standing before me. She looked a lot like Aengel, but her flaming orange hair tumbled all the way down to the floor and her eyes gleamed an unnatural shade of green. The white dress she was wearing was torn and smeared with dirt and blood. With wide eyes, I noticed that her skin had blood on it too.

"Are you hurt?" I tried to find where the blood was coming from, but it didn't seem to be hers...

"Sofiel!" She moved towards me arms outstretched. "I have be waiting for you for so long."

"What?" I blinked for a moment and then she was gone. "What?" I repeated to the empty space.

This is not right...

I started walking back to the others, gradually increasing my pace until I was sprinting like a madman down the tunnel.

Gotta get back. Gotta find them.

"Rabbit!" That voice- I knew that voice. Gruff, deep like any other orc's. "*Rabbit!*" I heard him right behind me.

I stopped and swung to clock him in the face as I spun around. Of course I missed.

"What the Hell do you *want*, Japeth!" I screamed at him. He grinned at me with his full grown tusks glinting against the dark. He was alone without his usual goons to beat me up. My entire childhood was spent under their fists until-

Until.

"You have something of mine, elf," he folded his massive arms across his chest. Suddenly I could feel every scar he ever gave me.

"What are you doing here, I-"

"Answer the question, fairy-boy."

I backed away from him. Like I always did.

I ran away from him, like before.

"YOU'RE NOT REAL! YOU'RE NOT REAL! YOU'RE NOT REAL!" I tore down the tunnel, desperate for this all to be just a nightmare. "AENGEL! AENGEL! LUCE! CZARA!" I was wheezing by the time I saw three figures running towards me.

I was shaking when we met in the middle of the tunnel so far under the ground.

"What happened to you?" Aengel put a gentle hand on my cheek, deeply concerned for my sanity. She quickly drew away once she realize she was touching me.

"I- I don't kn-know. I th-thought I saw a rat. I-I'mmm so-sorry." I shook uncontrollably as they all helped me onto the floor against a wall. Hugging my knees against my chest, I tried to tell them how I saw a rat and took a stroll down Horror Lane right by Hallucination Avenue. Luce checked me for any head trauma once I finished my story. It was the only explanation we had.

"How stupid are you?" Czara said. "What were you thinking going off alone like that?"

"Leave him alone," Aengel kneeled next to Luce in front of me. "Do you think it was a spell?" She asked him. I noticed something on her face, a streak of- of- oh God. Blood.

She looked at me, eyes black as death. "What's wrong, Rabbit?"

Screaming yanked me awake, and it took me a second to realize it was me who was screaming. Aengel, Luce, and Czara were shaking me and yelling over my screams for me to wake up. It was just a bad dream.

"I'm up! I'm up!" I shook them off me, deflecting their concerned looks.

"I rest my case," Czara said. "This is all just Mortis screwing with us."

"You okay?" Aengel helped me up, ignoring the fact that she had to touch me to do so.

I nodded.

"Luce," I said. "I know this places changes around, but start making a map so we can look for patterns."

He saluted. "I'm on it, boss."

"Czara, I want you keeping track of our food and water supply while we're down here. We should start rationing since we don't know when we'll get out of here."

"Or if," she said before opening up the backpacks and organizing the food and water.

Lastly, I turned to Aengel. "I need you to read my fortune."

She looked at me for a long moment, unsure how to respond.

"I don't like doing that, especially to people I know and I've done it to you at least twice."

"If there's a way to get out or something to avoid, the future would tell us that." And if it explains the nightmare still giving me chills, that'd be nice too.

"No," she shook her head, green eyes glinting. "You're not the one who seizes up and sees things normal people are blessed not to know. No, I don't want to. I might see you die like last time or I might just see an irrelevant memory- who knows: I know I don't want to."

"Fine, I'm not going to make you do anything."

"Good," she said.

It was a selfish idea anyways.

We spent a good while walking around and mapping out the tunnels. We kept track of things by having Czara mark the walls with her lipstick, which I was surprised she still had. We made several turns, drifting farther and farther away from any hope of making it out or finding the stupid animula to kill the stupid demon.

"Haven't we seen this tunnel before?" Aengel called from behind me.

"Probably," I said.

"We're going in circles," Luce sighed, nose stuck in the map he had been sketching as we walked.

"What's that?" Aengel said.

I turned around, "what?" She pointed to one of the walls a little farther ahead, directing our eyes to writing scribbled there on the stone. It looked like little flames with harsh lines struck through, I didn't recognize the language.

"It's draconic," I heard Czara say.

I gave her a look, not really sure how I wanted her to answer if I asked how she knew draconic, a language generally spoken by dragons and- yes- demons. I also wasn't sure if I wanted demon-speak written on any tunnel walls near me. Especially if I was trapped in that tunnel.

Just the same, I had to know what it said. "Can you read it?"

The half elf scoffed. "Can you tie your own boot? Or does Aengel do that for you too?"

"What are you-?"

"Shut up, I'm reading." She strode over to the writing and considered it thoughtfully.

Aengel gave her a searing glare. Luce and I took a step back a little.

"It says that we're getting close to what we came for but that it'll cost a-," she looked up at the writing for a second, "'-a fatal price'".

"Well that can't be good," I said.

Luce shook his golden head. "Nothing's ever good when it comes to demons."

"Except one thing." Czara smirked, looking Luce up and down. "But you probably didn't learn about that in seminary."

I gave her a look. *Typical Czara.*

"So, this is good," Aengel said. "It's helping us."

Luce shrugged. "Who knows?"

"Helps?" Czara laughed. "This just told us that one of us has to kill ourselves to get the stupid sword."

I chose not to hear her.

We followed the arrow under the writing deeper into the heart of the maze. The air got colder and soundless, begging us all to leave hope back it was warm and there was sun. I did my best to keep us moving with telling old elven children's stories that my mother used to tell me and scrapping the occasional joke- anything to keep from feeling like I was walking into my grave. Appalled by my corniness, Luce took over the joke department and did a worse job than I did. Aengel was amused, at the very least.

I was working on making my footsteps silent- a weird thing I do when I'm bored- when I started to smell something like a rotting cow. Not just that, but a rotting cow who had been killed three summer days earlier and had serious digestive problems in life and in death.

I sniffed, cringing immediately. "You guys smell that?"

Judging by their twisted up faces and hands covering their noses, they had.

"What is this?" Aengel's green eyes were watering.

I was about to answer, but stopped when I saw a part of the wall shimmer black for a fraction of a second and then-

"Run!" I roared.

We all sprinted forward before they could see the phantom clothed in ragged black robes peeling from the walls.

"Move! Move!" I shouted as Luce and Czara sprinted past me. Looking back, I saw Aengel lagging behind.

No.

She wasn't going to make it. The ghosts had practically reached her already and she was sprinting as fast as she knew how. I switched around and ran towards her just as the vapor-like hands grabbed her hair.

"Aengel!" The ghost had grabbed her neck and was draining the life out of her, growing as it did so. "Let her go!" I took a swing at the apparition, only to go right through the black mist. "*Let her go!*" My roar shook the walls, echoing to the ends of the maze and beyond. The ghost disappeared, leaving Aengel in a crumpled heap on the floor.

"Aengel?" I sank to my knees, an anchor of dread sunk to the bottom of my stomach. I picked her up like a baby, her limp arms scraped the floor as I pulled her close. "Can you hear me?" She was breathing, but barely. Luce and Czara were beside me suddenly.

"That was a demon," Luce said it like he was talking to himself.

"It didn't look like one," I never took my eyes off her, afraid that she'd stop breathing if I did.

"There's lots of kinds of demons," he sneaked a glance at Czara

"What can we do?" I said, cradling her head.

He shook his head. "I don't know."

Czara said nothing. She just stared blankly at the pale face of her only friend.

"We need to keep moving," she said at last. I nodded and I trailed behind carrying the unconscious Aengel. That was when I began to ask myself why we were even bothering with this anymore.

Chapter 27

It's easy to lose hope when you can't see the sun. Especially if you've been underground for over 48 hours and have to carry the unconscious body of one of your friends through the dark tunnels, knowing one of you'll have to die anyways. As we got closer, Czara offered some comfort that she might be able to raise the sacrifice back to life, but only as an undead creature. You can't win.

I was actually pretty surprised how easy the rest of the maze was from then on, besides the fact, of course, I was carrying around Aengel's dead weight. It was as if something, or someone, wanted us to find the sword. Exhausted and worn through, we shuffled on following the writing on the wall and hoped that it wouldn't lead us astray. I called a lunch break, the last of our food, at the last possible minute when all of our stomachs were growling enough to echo through the halls.

A soft groan drifted from Aengel when I laid her on the ground. I took it as a sign that she was healing.

I turned to Czara while she was pulling out the food. "Can't you work some of your warlock-magic on her?"

She could hardly look at her friend.

"I'm not a healer."

"She'll heal on her own in time," Luce said. He sat himself beside me and we shared the last of his walnuts. My stomach protested, nuts were not enough to live on. I couldn't remember the last time I had a decent meal or rest. I'd been so on edge and uncomfortable for so long, my nerves were starting to fray. Aengel looked almost at peace laying there on the floor. Her shallow breaths moved her chest up and down ever so slightly just to let me know she was still alive. Her flaming red hair fanned around her face like a fiery halo, making her name seem even more fitting than when I first met that fortune-telling girl in the slums of Shatterpoole. I remembered how she couldn't stop fussing with her hair when we were on our way to the Antimarx's masquerade, when we bumped into each other in their dungeon. I looked at her and saw her face the second she recognized me through the blood in the werewolf village, and the awe in her eyes as we watched the lights dance across the sky in our stolen sleigh.

I slid my hand into hers.

Luce and Czara looked at me. I ignored them. The stone walls crumbled away and the all hunger and aches that wracked my body faded.

I looked at her and I could see that raw, searing second when she told me what a cupidon curse was.

I knew it was real.

Her fingers moved slowly to curl around mine.

"She moved!" I smiled uncontrollably.

"Well, she was never *dead*," Luce said. "But this is an improvement."

Czara smiled at me naughtily. "I told you so."

Aengel's eyes dragged open, slowly shifted her head back and forth to shake off the sleep.

She looked confused when she realized where she was. "What happened?"

"You got attacked by a demon," Luce blurted out.

"Oh," she said, closing her eyes again. "Well that's good news."

"You're lucky," Czara smirked. "I was hoping to test out my reanimation skills before we one of us goes all noble on the sacrifice table."

We all looked at her.

She shrugged. "Hey, you gotta do what you gotta do."

Aengel grabbed her head and squeezed her eyes shut.

"You want anything to eat?" I said.

"Got any toast?"

"No, but we have some walnuts."

She moved her head to look at me sitting next her. "That it?"

"Unfortunately."

With some effort, she managed to sit up and take the bag from me. It was the longest lunch break we'd had, and I knew we needed to keep moving. With the path so clear now, I wasn't so sure I actually even wanted to find the animula. One of us had to kill ourselves for it and I knew I couldn't let that be Aengel. Luce might volunteer himself, but he's hardly gotten the chance to live already. He'd been stuck in a monastery his entire life and he shouldn't go and die now that he's finally out. Czara wouldn't volunteer, she'd be the one holding the sword.

We only walked for a little bit more after that. Aengel was still weak, but insisted that she didn't need to be carried. It was probably more out of fear of getting a vision rather than pride. Czara was first to see the door.

"Found it," she smirked back at us triumphantly.

It was a massive iron door engraved with the fiery demon script that led us here. Dread knotted my stomach. I felt like hurling. Wasn't this supposed to be our moment of victory? We pushed open the door easily, despite its size. It revealed a large stone room with only the center furnished with a cold stone altar.

And a knife.

Aengel was the first to speak. "Wasn't the animula a sword?"

"That's why we need a sacrifice," Luce said coldly. He must've been just as nervous as the rest of us.

"Don't all raise your hands at once," Czara said. "I hope you're each aware I can raise people from the dead."

"But there's a catch," Aengel mumbled to herself, gaze fixed on the smooth, plain dagger. We all lingered by the door, no one wanted to get too close.

"Well, you'll be a vampire when you wake up, but hey, you won't be dead."

"Vampires are technically dead," the ex-priest said.

A long, silent moment passed. Light came from a simple hole in the tall ceiling, making the blade of the dagger glint at us eagerly. I just wanted the bastard dead. If I had to die to kill Mortis, so be it.

"I'll do it," I finally said.

Czara rolled her eyes, "didn't see that one coming."

"Stop," Aengel glared at her. "This is serious- he's going to kill himself."

She threw her hands up, "no need, I'll do it for him." She strode over to me and dragged me to the altar by my collar and picked up the dagger. "He'd chicken out if we let him play with the knife by himself."

"No I wo-"

She plunged the dagger into my heart before I even saw her arm move. There was a faint smile on her lips as my vision faded and my body sank to the floor. The last sounds I heard were Aengel and Luce yelling something about a heartless bitch.

And then there was nothing.

At first there was black. I could only know there was darkness because it wrapped around my consciousness like an endless dark ocean, its waters black and lifeless.

Nothing.

Nothing.

There is no heaven or hell for orcs or elves.

Or me.

"Hey, he's opening his eyes."

"See, I told you he'd be fine."

"Um, he's still undead."

"Shut up priest, nobody asked you."

"You shut up, he's coming to."

I forced my eyelids open and found them all standing over me. Czara was holding the sword that had just been the dagger, its steel soaked with blood. My blood.

"Did it work?" I choked out. I felt weird all over. It was like my blood had turned cold and my-

My heart wasn't beating.

I shot up and put a hand on my chest. Nothing.

I checked to see if I was even breathing.

No.

Then I noticed my skin. Remember how it was deep forest green? I gapped at its ghostly paleness. I was practically the same color as the ginger.

"Hey, I- I, um- something isn't right. I-"

Aengel kneeled beside me as I sat there realizing exactly how dead I was.

"It feels weird."

"You'll be fine," Luce forced a smile. "Just think, now you can smell better, run better, and heal faster-"

"I could already heal fast," I said. "How will I see the sun again? What happens when I get hungry?"

"I can put a charm on you and we'll find you a cow," Czara said. "Don't worry about it." She was being nice for once.

"And oh yeah," she said, icy blue eyes glinting. "Aengel can't tell you're fortunes now, but that'll work out for the best I'm sure. Besides, you can pass for a giant human with two extra-long teeth on your bottom jaw."

Aengel's cheeks flushed red.

The half elf shrugged. "I'm just saying."

A rock fell from the ceiling, making us all jump as it crashed to the floor on the other side of the room. I stood up and we all looked to the ceiling. Soft morning light beamed down on us making my skin burn.

"I think now is a good time for that charm you were talking about," I said, my skin started blister.

"Indeed," she grabbed my face and mumbled a few strange words. Glorious warm coursed through me and then I was cold again. "You should be good now."

"Thanks," no sooner had I said it when another rock fell. This time Luce had to jump out of its way. We all looked at each other. Czara picked up the animula sword and handed it to Luce to replace his old sword in his scabbard. His old sword was crap anyways. The walls were crumbling and we had to scramble to dodge the raining chunks of rock.

"Get over here, Eli! Luce!" Czara grabbed onto Aengel and stretched her arms to hold us all together.

"What are you doing?" I said. Aengel was starting to go pale and her eyes were unfocused.

"Czara?" Luce tried to pull away.

"Shut up guys, I'm getting us out of here." She closed her eyes and bowed her head. Her lips moved but no sound came out.

I blinked.

Chapter 28

We were standing back in the woods in the clearing where I found the entrance to the tunnel. Our horses were gone and a blanket of snow covered the ground and trees.

Czara let go of us and sank to the ground. Luce grabbed her, and I grabbed Aengel before she fell over from her vision.

Czara shook him off. "Thanks but no thanks, priest."

Aengel slowly regained focus and told Luce not to eat any strange plants in the near future.

"I'd be glad to eat anything at this point," he sighed.

"We should figure out what the closest town is and hoof it over there. Hopefully there'll be an inn or something where we can reset in. I think we could all use a break from the road for at least a couple days."

"How are we going to pay for that?" Aengel said sorely. A barmaid's salary didn't cover much, and fortune telling didn't help much either.

"Peasants," Czara waved a bejeweled hand. "I can pay for it." We all thanked her, begrudgingly, and followed Luce as he directed us to a dot on the map not too far from where we thought we were.

By high noon we were all dehydrated and starving. We had resorted to eating snow to keep from passing out. I wasn't sure if the smell of dying horse was all of us, or just me. The lack of blood pumping through me began to be an obnoxiously loud silence.

We walked.

And walked.

And walked.

And then some more walking.

"Luce!" I groaned. "How close are we?"

"Not much farther. Maybe a mile or two if I have our location right."

He didn't

My head pounded and my lips were cracked. Suddenly I noticed something in the air. It smelled like a juicy, rare steak. It wasn't one of those crappy steaks you get at the cheap inns. No, this was the kind you'd think a king would get on his golden feast table. My mouth began to water. New beads of sweat glistened on my moon-pale skin.

Aengel was looked at me, concern clear on her face. "Eli?"

All I could see was the red, hot blood shooting through her. She must've stepped back, because I stepped forward.

"Eli? Eli!" I only heard her through a haze. I lost control, I couldn't see, I couldn't feel, I could only smell the blood.

Her blood.

A bolt of lightning shot through me, sending me crashing to the ground. I shook uncontrollably for a good minute, electricity shooting through me.

"We are friends, not food." Czara stood over me with her arms folded. She playfully kicked me in the head to make sure I was conscious. I was, surprisingly. One of my vampire perks I guess. I stood up and tried to shake off the hunger long enough to apologize for almost eating Aengel. She accepted. Reluctantly.

"Before you kill someone," Luce said. "Why don't you go find a rabbit or something? There has to be a warm blooded animal in these woods besides us."

Maybe I said "okay", maybe I didn't. I just got away from them as fast as possible. And kept running.

I grabbed onto a tree and sank to my knees in the snow, resting my face against the dead bark.

I almost killed her-I almost killed her-I almost killed her! Of all the people? Why Aengel? Why not Czara-

A pebbled nicked me in the back of the head, snapping me out of my self-pity party.

"Keep moving orc, you won't last long on an empty stomach and neither will we," Czara had followed me.

"What are you doing here, Czara?"

"Making sure you don't chicken out on the rabbit and then go all feral on Aengel again later. Or me. Mostly me."

"I don't need a babysitter to watch me eat."

She strode over to me and pulled me up. "You're a vampire now, in case you haven't noticed. Unless you've been one before it's safe to say you don't know how to eat like one."

I didn't answer, I just shook her off me and tried to walk away. My head was pounding again and all I could smell, see, feel, was the red pumping through her.

"Stop looking at me like that, I *will* shock you."

I glared at her through the fog. It started closing around me, all I could see was her veins and arteries beating with life. I needed it.

"*Ow!*" The electricity buzzed through me effortlessly. "Stop doing that!"

"And let you eat me? I think *not*."

"I'm *hungry!*"

The bushes beside us started to rustle and a rabbit skittered into view and then out again once he realized he was interrupting.

I blacked out.

When my mind caught up with my body again, I had a rabbit carcass shoved in my face and its warm blood dripping down my throat and my chest.

"What?" I dropped the rabbit. She was smiling.

"I'm glad you're embracing it. I wish I could show you what you look like, but seeing that you don't have a reflection I guess I'll just have to enjoy the view for myself."

I wish I felt sick, but I was just hungry. I found two more rabbits and a squirrel before Czara agreed to bring me back to Luce and Czara. She wanted to be sure I was safe to be around warm blooded creature who can't defend themselves so easily. Aengel's a delicate girl and Luce could only stun me with his light trick.

We walked back in silence. The wet blood all over me should've made me cold in the chilly afternoon air, but it didn't. I was dead. Aengel didn't look at me when we kept walking to the village. She didn't say a word. It was almost evening by the time we reached a trading post town. Luce confirmed that we were, indeed heading west and deeper into the kingdom. I had only ever lived on the coast, the thought of being completely surrounded by land almost unnerved me. When we saw the lights of the town as the sun started setting early for winter.

I stopped. "I can't walk in like this."

Each considered me for a moment, noting that I was covered in blood from my mouth to my belt.

"Wait," Luce threw off his backpack and started digging through it. "I have your 'poncho' you made from the horse blanket. You can wash up with the snow and then we'll just throw this over you."

I nodded and grabbed some snow to start scrubbing my face, luckily I had no feeling anymore. He threw me the horse blanket and I pulled it on.

Aengel couldn't help but break a smile. "You look ridiculous."

I looked down. Tribal wasn't exactly my style. I smiled back. Just the fact that she was looking at me again was enough.

The town guard let us in even though the sun had gone down and the gates had closed. This was weird, but I chalked it up on it being a good day to be alive- that is, if I wasn't dead. There were still people out in the streets, lit by the warm glow of street lanterns. It started to snow a little, but not enough to stick. I saw Aengel shiver, and would've given her my poncho if it wasn't covering all the blood on me. Truth be told, I wasn't cold. I wasn't warm either. We found a nice inn and Czara insisted we get the suite. And room service. I didn't mind, she was paying for it anyways.

We were standing in the lobby of the inn waiting for our room when Aengel elbowed me in the ribs.

"Did you see the way everyone's looking at you?"

"What?"

She shook her head and smiled.

Czara scooted beside me. "Being a vampire gets you extra pretty-boy points. You're like a big, pale human with supernatural good looks and teeny-tiny tusks. Best thing that ever happened to you."

I looked at them both as they smiled goofily at me.

I swept my eyes around the room and my suspicions were confirmed when most of the girls in the lobby caught my eye and then jerked their heads in the opposite direction.

"Oh."

Finally the bellhop came back with our room key and escorted us to the suite with a smile. We walked in and it was like walking into a palace apartment. Three of us gaped in awe at the opulence of it all. One of us allowed satisfied smile. The door led into a large salon with couches and a grand fireplace. Four doors came off of the room, we each picked one and found master bedrooms in each. Mine had a giant, satin-covered bed in the center with red velvet pillows covering half of it and a blood red veil hanging over it. The room had its own fireplace, and a screen with a copper bathtub behind it. I took off my boots and just walked around a bit on the fur rugs, enjoying their fuzziness a little too much. At least I still had a sense of touch. Czara ordered us all a bath and then a dinner in the living room afterwards. I kept my poncho on as the servant, a large middle-aged man dressed in a black formal uniform, filled up the tub and left me a basket of soaps and scrubs and a ridiculously fluffy towel. Apparently she had also ordered me new clothes, because the servant brought me a new set of clothes: a wine colored button-up shirt, black dress pants with suspenders, a black waist coat, and a dinner jacket. New socks and boxers too. She never misses a thing, does she? The man eyed my poncho as he handed me the clothes and then left the room without a word.

"Thanks!" I called after him. Who knows if he really heard me though, he was very eager to get away. I smelled like death itself, never mind the fact that I was, indeed dead.

If the water was warm, I didn't notice. It was weird getting over the fact that I couldn't feel temperature anymore. It was even weirder looking in the mirror and seeing no one looking back. It took a while, but I finally managed to get myself squeaky clean and dressed up well enough to meet the queen herself. All I needed was a top hat and a fancy cane. Every vampire needs a cane sword.

The dinner was marvelous. I was even more excited to find that I still could enjoy human food even though all I craved was blood.

It took me a while to fall asleep. The night was my new day and my new body didn't want to stay in bed during it. Eventually the exhaustion from the past few days took over and I drifted off.

Chapter 29

I woke up in the small hours of the morning when it was still dark outside. Sleep didn't seem all that appealing and I didn't feel like getting out of my room. That meant I would've had to make myself look presentable, and it was too early for that. I rolled out of bed and kneeled on the floor to look under it. Carefully, I closed my hand around the hidden object underneath.

The animula.

The hilt seemed to recognize my fingers as I closed my hand around the grooved metal. Luce gave it to me last night to keep safe. I could see it perfectly in the darkness. Its blade was flawless steel and its hilt was engraved with knotted symbols the Ancients decorated everything with. Except, except it was lacking. The pattern of the knots seemed to focus around a center point on the guard, but the center point was just a hole. It was like something was missing, like a jewel or a bolt. I looked at it for a little longer, wondering if anything else looked like it was missing until I heard movement in the common room. I already had pants and an undershirt on, so I didn't bother going full dress code to see what the noise was.

"Look who's up and gracing the world with his newfound beauty?"

Czara.

"Good morning," I drew back into my room and quickly shut the door. Being a vampire didn't matter about when it was too early in the morning to see *her*. Especially if she was going to make comments.

I waited until I heard Luce's voice in the living room before I went back out. Maybe she wouldn't make some awkward remark about my looks with him around. He was considered pretty up there, I think, so that evens out the field a little.

"Hello handsome."

Why? Why me?

"Good morning," I plucked up a pastry from the plate on the tea cart that a servant must've brought in and flopped down on the couch next to Luce, who was already well into his croissant.

"Hey," he said behind his food.

"Hey."

I looked around for a second once I finished my flaky-delight. "Where's Aengel?"

Czara pointed to the bedroom. "She's still getting over almost dying and all. Not from you, from the demon."

"Is she going to be okay?"

"She just needs to sleep it off," Luce said from the couch. "I've run into one of those buggers before. I was trying to study their behavior, and that's when I figured field work wasn't for me. It got me three days of sleep though, which was awesome."

"But she'll be fine, right?"

Luce nodded. "Oh yeah, she'll be running around and prophesying people in no time."

Looking at the wooden door between us, and I wondered if any of it was my fault. I mean, I had almost killed her. Surely she'd feel at least a little tempted to avoid me. I would've. Czara announced that she was going into town to go buy some supplies for our trip back to Shatterpoole where we'd find someone to teach me combat skills. We had to kill him with the sword, and at present, none of us were ready to take on a greater demon with a hunk of steel between us- magical or not. It was me who would kill him, although Czara would've been more than happy to. Not only was I already dead anyways, but I was also the biggest, strongest, and the whole urgency in killing him was so *I* don't have to raise his demon army.

Luce went with her. I volunteered to stay in the suite to guard the sword and Aengel. Sitting on the couch, I grabbed a spoon from the tea cart with the pastries on it, and tried to catch my reflection in it. So the stories were true for once. No reflection. Without a mirror I already knew I looked fairly human, if you ignored the teeth and the pointed ears. Sure I was a big guy, but humans can get pretty big. Half elves don't, so I couldn't pass as one of them any more than I could back when I was green. I wondered if my eyes were even blue anymore.

"Where is everyone?" Aengel stepped out of her room and was looking curiously around the salon. She wrapped a blanket around her shoulders and shuffled over to the tea cart.

"They went to go get some stuff, they should be back before lunch," I called over from the couch.

She plopped down next to me and started nibbling on a pastry. She looked paler than usual, and her hair was in even more wild waves than usual around her face. Dark circles underlined her eyes. I hadn't noticed them before.

"How you feeling?"

She didn't look up from her breakfast. "Like crap."

"Luce said you should be fine in a couple days, all you can do is sleep it off. Once you're feeling better we can start heading back to Shatterpoole," I said.

She shivered. I got up to poke the fire back to life when a loud knock shook the door.

"Open up!" It was a man's voice.

"Hold on!" I called back. Aengel was grabbing her head as the knocking continued. Louder this time, and more urgently.

"You need to get in your room before someone comes in, can you walk?" The banging filled the room, and she looked like her head was about to explode. Before wasting any more time, I scooped her up and ran her into her room before yanking the door open.

"*What?*" I growled.

I wouldn't know what he looked like, because he was standing there in a priest's uniform, the same one that Luce used to wear: a plague doctor's dress code, except with dirty white cloth.

"Do you know the whereabouts of Brother Lucifer Ornias of the Order of Mortis?"

I looked at him blankly for a moment before I realized he was talking about Luce. Shaking my head, I said, "nope, no idea who that is. Who are *you*?"

He stood up a bit straighter and declared in practiced tempo, "I am Brother Paymon Malphas, the boy I am looking for went missing while in my charge."

"Sounds like a personal issue," I went to slam the door. He grabbed it with amazing strength, strong enough to equal my orc-elf-vampire self. "Let go."

"I'm going to search your rooms," he started to push past me. I pushed back.

"No. I have no idea who you're looking for, and I'm not letting you search my rooms." I leaned into the eye holes of the mask, almost close enough to let the long beak poke me in the chest. "Leave."

"I know who you are, Son of Fair and Foul. You may look like a man, but I can smell the monster in your blood."

I threw my weight against the door, crushing his gloved hand as well as the door frame. A cry came from the other side of the wood as I pressed myself against it and scored my mind for what to do next. He started pounding on the door, forcing me to push even harder.

If I move and he opens the door, I'm screwed. If I stay here and do nothing, I'll still get screwed somehow.

Aengel's door opened and she peeked her head out. When she saw me barricading the door and waving her back into her room, she shook her head and hobbled over to the fire place.

What are you doing? I mouthed when she looked up to see me still holding off the pounding. For now. She gave a small smile and showed me the white hot poker she pulled out of the embers. Silently, she handed placed it in my hand and shuffled back to her room as fast as her drained little legs could carry her.

I counted backwards from five. I heard the wood splinter.

The second I sprang away from the door, the door split and the priest bounded inside the room with amazing speed. This guy wasn't human. Immediately I swung the fire poker at him. And missed. He swung back with his clothed fist, me jumping out of the way just in time. Both of us had some supernatural aid on our side. That much was obvious. Our swings and punches were lightning fast, moving at a speed faster than I could think.

But let's face it, the only fights I'd ever been in were with the boys back home.

He connected with my ribs, sending me out of rhythm. It was downhill from there when my utter lack of experience came back to bite me. I was on the ground in a second, getting kicked faster than I could heal.

But I was undead, and he wasn't.

I felt the canines in the top row of my teeth stretching and poking into my lip.

He paused for half a second, and I was back on my feet. In the back of my mind, I prayed Aengel was hidden or escaped in case this ended poorly. I grabbed his hood mask and tore it off him, my fist grabbing a handful of golden hair. Without heeding the black eyes bulging at me, I sank my fangs into his pale neck and mauled into the flesh. He squirmed like a worm on a hook, but I did not let go. His blood tasted sour and thick. I sucked it out of him like a massive leech. I drank and I drank until the squirming stopped and long after that. I drank until every last drop of color was drained from him and his veins had shrunk up and gone dry.

Throwing down his body, I felt stronger. I could sense his blood seeping through tissue and for the first time since I died, I could feel the December air drafting in the room. I wasn't sure whether to be jumping up and down because I could feel hot and cold again, or horrified because I had just literally sucked the life out of a man to do so. I went with the jumping, He was trying to kill me anyways. Besides, several signs pointed to him not being a man in the first place. By no means was he a woman, but he certainly wasn't human. His blood didn't smell like one. Humans have an earthy smell to them, he smelled like an old book nobody wanted to read for the past hundred years. I didn't know what kind of creature could smell like *that*.

"You can come out now, Aengel." I gave the body a good kick just to make sure he was as dead as I hoped he was. "Aengel?"

Her door creaked open and she slipped out, hugging the blanket around her thin frame.

"Is he dead?" She studied the body curiously.

I nodded, "You don't look so good, maybe you should get back to bed. Luce said you're supposed to sleep this off."

"I can't sleep," she said. "Not last night, not today." Her eyes were fixed on the corpse, but I had a feeling she wasn't seeing him at all.

"If you want to try sleeping on the couch, you'll be closer to the fire."

"Okay," she sunk down into the soft fabric of the couch. "Will you stay with me?" Her eyes were desperate.

I nodded.

Before I went to go sit by the fire, I went to go grab another blanket for her off her bed. By the time we had her all snuggled down and I had moved the body into my bathtub and tied it up with some bed sheets for good measure, I sat on the floor by her head facing the fire. This was the night at the ice castle all over again, except so much had happened since then.

"Do you know any stories?" she mumbled to me.

"Only the elven kind my mother used to tell me."

"Will you tell me one?"

I kept my eyes on the fire, entranced by the sharp, graceful movement of the flames. "Sure. Let's see, huh. Well, long ago there lived a little elf who had silver hair and stars for eyes..."

Chapter 30

Aengel was fast asleep by the time Luce and Czara got back. I went back and forth from my spot by the couch to check on the priest lying dead in my bathtub and the common room. In the back of my mind I had this fear that he'd reanimate somehow. Although, he must be some priest if he can come back from having all his blood drained and part of his throat ripped out. To pass the time when I wasn't making sure the dead guy was still dead, I worked on craving a hunk of wood that came off the door when the late Brother Paymon went raging bull against it. I borrowed one of Czara's knives she'd left out on her dresser even though I was sure she wouldn't be too happy about that. It turned out to be a little feather that could be a necklace charm.

I was nicking the final details when someone pushed the door open. Czara stuck her head in and examined the damaged on the door.

"Care to explain this one, orc?"

I stood up and pointed a finger at Aengel sleeping, pressing a finger to my lips. Luce came in, bumping into the half elf. She gave him a harsh shush and plowed over to her room, ushering me with her. Luce dropped the new packs he was carrying by the door before following us into the room.

I shut the door before I explained that a priest looking for Luce had come by. And tried to kill me.

"What happened to him?" Luce said curiously.

"He's in my room."

Czara's eyes widened. "You left him alone?"

I shook my head, "he's dead, I think that's okay."

They shared and look and then nodded.

"What did he say?" Luce asked. "Why was he looking for me, did he tell you?"

"I don't really know," I said. "He was too busy trying to kill me to chat."

Luce ran his hands through his hair and started pacing frantically around Czara's bedroom.

"Should we be concerned?" Czara said.

"I don't know, I don't know..." He kept his eyes fixed on the floor as he stormed back and forth.

"Luce," I reached out a hand to hold him still. "Is everything okay?"

He stopped and looked up at me with horror teeming through the blue of his eyes.

"They're coming for me."

Breath shallow and skin pale, he repeated again, "they're coming for me."

"Who?" I let go of him even though I was afraid he'd fall over. He looked so pale.

"The- the priests. My order. I should've known- you can't just walk away from them like that. No, I should've known, I-"

Czara backhanded him, sending him stumbling back. "Stop muttering to yourself like that. It's annoying. And useless."

I gave her a look. The guy was freaked out, cut him some slack. She was clearly nervous too.

"Luce," I said calmly. "Who exactly is it that we should be worried about. I don't care about the why at this point."

He folded his arms in front of him, to keep from shaking I supposed. "When you join a priest order, you become more than family, you become a brotherhood. When I left, I broke a sacred vow. That's punishable by death. Even worse, I left to help kill Mortis, who happens to be the patron of my order. Whatever they do to me now will be worse than death."

Something about him looked hollow.

"Well, I took care of this guy," I said. "But something tells me more will come. Obviously they know where we are now so we should probably cut the vacation short and get moving again."

Luce shook his head. "We can't move Aengel so soon. Getting here had put her on bedrest, getting back on the road might kill her. You two might not know this, but life-draining vampires tend to be very effective in what they do."

Czara sighed. "We can't leave her behind."

"Maybe I could carry her," I suggested. "I can't trigger visions and she's light enough. The only danger would be me getting hungry."

Luce nodded, "yeah, that could work."

"Oh come, come, E. We all know you just want some cuddle time with the pretty redhead."

I raised an eyebrow. "E?"

She tossed her hair on me as she walked by. "It's you're new nickname." Luce and I shared a look as we walked back into the salon. Aengel was moving around on the couch, so I decided to go over to check on her and make sure she was comfortable enough. She looked paler, if that was even possible, and she was shivering despite the fact she had enough blankets to supply the Queen's army on top of her. Aware my faulty temperature-feeling, I asked Czara to check Aengel's forehead for any fever.

"Good lord, she's on fire."

I kneeled down next to her head and carefully put a hand on her shoulder to wake her up. I hesitated for a second, realizing how our skin almost matched.

"Aengel?" I shook her gently. "Hey, Aengel?"

Her eyes dragged open, taking a moment to focus on me. "Hi," she mumbled.

"You have a high fever and you're not well, but we need to move you soon. I need your consent to treat it, however weird it sounds."

"Just don't touch me," she muttered before hazing over from the fever.

I turned to Czara. "Go to the kitchen and get some uncooked potatoes, a dish rag, and vinegar."

She took off out the splintered door.

"Luce," he looked at me, fear still unfaded in his eyes. "Go get us ready to move. Pack up the stuff, and find some food." He nodded and went over to the new packs he and Czara had bought that morning. "And Luce!" I called over to him. "Get her some water please!"

"On it, boss!" He rushed out of the room in search of a servant.

I looked back at her when she moaned. I didn't need to feel hot or cold to tell how high her temperature was. I peeled the blankets off of her and pulled her into my arms and carried her back to her room. She was too close to the fire, which was not helping her body cool down at all. In fact, it had the opposite effect. Her night dress was stuck to her with sweat and her breaths came out quick and shallow. Laying her down on the bed gently, I pull the blankets away from her and opened up her window to let in the winter chill.

If we could at least get her temperature down to a manageable level, we could probably move her before the fever goes. I mean, it was cold enough outside. I went and grabbed Czara's knife I borrowed earlier from by the fire place.

Luce came in and found us back in Aengel's room, pitcher of water in hand. Czara was right behind him with a large bowl of potatoes and a bottle of vinegar.

I told Czara to get Aengel to drink and Luce to help me cut these potatoes. We dumped out the bowl and poured the vinegar in, dropping in the potato slices we cut as we went along. After letting the slices soak for a few minutes, I told Czara to stop forcing water down the poor girl's throat and to cover her skin in the potato slices.

"What?"

I pointed to the bowl. "We have to get her temperature down. Luce and I will leave the room, so no need to get weird about it."

The half elf slammed the door behind us, leaving me with nothing to do but help Luce pack us up. The new backpacks we complete with bedrolls, preserved food, water canteens, matches, knives, and a little boo-boo kit with bandages and gauze.

Yes, a boo-boo kit.

It didn't take us long to get three packs by the door and ready to go. The other pack was in Czara's room, but we obviously couldn't go in there. The only thing left to deal with was, well, the dead body in my bathtub. Luce and I stood over him, trying to figure out what to do.

"We could burn him."

I shook my head. "Wouldn't that take too long?"

"Not if we have Czara do it. Cremation is against the priest code, I say we go with that."

I met his eyes with mine. "You really hate him, don't you?"

"Him," Luce glared at the corpse. "And everything he ever stood for." He stormed out of the room, getting away from his former brother as fast as humanly possible. I stayed though, still watching the dead priest. All of his color was gone, and he had this waxy look about him that made him look even more dead. It was his eyes that bothered me. They were black- not dark brown, or extra dark blue- just black. Surely that wasn't normal. Plus, as far as I knew, judging by his golden hair and complexion (before he died, obviously), his eyes should've been light blue like Luce's. I pulled out the animula sword from under the bed went after the ex-priest.

"Hey," I handed him the sword to put in his scabbard. It would've been too obvious to Mortis if I was carrying it, and honestly I just didn't want to carry it. He was sitting on the couch and narrowing his eyes at the fire. "What was up with the dead guy's eyes?"

He turned around on his knees to face me. "That's from a dedication ceremony, all the older priests have eyes like that."

"How come you don't?" I ventured.

He turned back around. "I missed my ceremony, on purpose."

"Is that why you came with us?"

"That's certainly part of it."

He looked agitated as is, so I stopped the questions and went to check on the girls. Knocking on the door, I called to ask how Aengel was holding up. Czara opened the door a crack, peeking one icy eye out.

"Fever's down, smells like vinegar and potatoes. Anything else?"

"No. Thanks, Czara."

The eye narrowed. "Anytime."

"Get her ready to move, I want to get out of here in ten minutes."

The door closed, but I heard a "yes, master" from inside. Ignoring it, but enjoying the authority, I sat with Luce. Us guys were ready to go, we just needed Aengel to be ready too.

"Do we have horses?" I asked him.

"Yeah, Czara got us some this morning. I call the gray one, by the way."

Something just puzzled me. "Where is she getting all this money?"

"She didn't tell you?"

"No." Why would she tell me anything?

"Aengel didn't either?"

"What are you talking about? The apothecary thing?"

"Right," Luce said. "Well, she's an apothecary who sells narcotics to the Antimarx for the upper-class. She's popular with the lower class too, I hear. Aengel was her business partner until Czara screwed over the Antimarx and got them both on the hit list."

"What? How do you know all this?" I knew this, but I'm surprised he did too.

He shrugged. "She did a lot of talking when we were stuck back at the Mortis house and when we were trying to find you and Aengel." He threw his hands up, "I have no idea why she told me that, so don't ask."

"No one can know why Czara does what Czara does." The story did make sense. It certainly explained why the Veit Antimarx and his henchman, Wace, came into the Blue Bear that day, and why Wace came back later for her. It also explained why she wouldn't tell me. Who wants to go around admitting their involvement in the drug trade? Not anyone who wanted to protect their reputation.

"Ready." Luce and I jumped up to see Czara standing by Aengel's bedroom door, hands on hips. Aengel stumbled out behind her, dressed in her black adventure gear again, but pale as ever.

"Ready," she forced.

We went to pick up our packs, I grabbed two.

"I can carry my own," she jutted her sharp chin up at me.

"I know you can, but you don't have to," I said. She heaved a frustrated sigh and followed Luce and Czara out the splintered door.

"Wait!" I said. "What about the body?"

Czara threw down her backpack and stormed back into the room. When we caught up with her, she had already started pouring her canteen on the guy.

She struck a match.

"You guys'd like to think that was water." She dropped the little flame, and we watched in horror as the body was engulfed in fire the second it hit him.

"So you're drinking lighter fluid now?" Aengel said.

"Hasn't killed me yet." There was that smirk.

Suddenly everyone noticed that there was a person-bonfire in the room and we cleared out pretty quickly.

I hesitated. "We can't just leave him burning like that, it'll set the room on fire."

"We can't risk people finding him," Luce said.

I knew he was right, and led the way down the hall, the stairs, and out the front door. On the stairs, I made sure to scream *"FIRE!"* sending everyone in the building besides Aengel, Luce, and Czara into panic. We three walked out of the inn full of smoke and screaming and got over to the stables. Almost everyone was mounted and ready to go, except Aengel, who was still too weak from the other vampire attack. I dismounted and went over to her.

"Are you going to ride with one of us, or are you going to try to ride by yourself and fall off and crack your head open?" We had just set a building on fire. It was not the time to argue about her independence.

"I'm fine," she shoved back some red hair. "I just need a boost."

I didn't want her passing out from riding when she was barely conscious that morning, but she didn't want to not kill herself apparently.

I dismounted and helped her on her own horse. "Just promise me you'll keep drinking your water."

"I will," she spurred the horse forward. I hopped back on mine and followed her out of the stable with the rest of us.

Chapter 31

We rode for about ten minutes before Aengel almost fell off her horse. Exhaustion doesn't ride well apparently. Defeated, I pulled her up on my horse and tied her horse's lead to mine. I knew it was a bad idea in the first place. Winter had already come, making the forest we were riding through look like a white wonderland. Without leaves for the wind to rustle, the only sounds came from the birds up in the bare trees and our horses clomping down the snowy path. The plan was to get back to Shatterpoole and find the swordsman Czara thought could teach me to kill demons, and to make sure Aengel didn't die on the way. I only needed to kill one demon, but unfortunately he was one of the hardest to get rid of. We had the sword, all we needed now was the skill.

The woods were getting thicker, narrowing the path to one horse's width. Luce led the way as our navigator with me and Aengel close behind. Czara trailed behind us, working on rationing what was left in her canteen. The ride to Shatterpoole was about two days from where we were, and the towns in between would be spotty on her poison of choice. Maybe it was the vampirism, but I noticed Luce's movements were a little more jerky than usual and I could hear his blood shooting through him. He smelled like fear. I called for a rest, saying Aengel needed a break despite her protests. Czara and Aengel got into a conversation about how thick men were, or something, so I took the chance to take Luce aside.

"Hey, do you have a minute?"

He looked at me, looking surprised. "Sure."

We stepped away from the girls out of earshot. I tried to phrase this right without looking like a softie or a paranoid.

"Are you okay?" I said.

He tilted his head up to look me in the eyes. "I'm fine."

He certainly didn't seem fine, and I told him so.

"I'm just not enjoying that every second we get closer to my monastery is every second we get closer to the priests finding me."

"Don't worry," I gave him a good pat on the back, sending him a bit forward. "We'll take care of you."

The girls gave us looks when we walked back over to them, but said nothing as we mounted up and got back on the road. My talk with Luce seemed to have done nothing for his nerves. If anything, he was worse. I even saw beads of sweat collecting under his hairline.

Aengel rode in front of me on the horse so I could grab onto her if she started to fall off. We were lucky her fever stayed down and she was starting to get some energy back. It was almost sunset, what a difference a day can make. Only that morning she was hardly able to get out of bed. It was no problem controlling the horse from behind her because she was so small. I could easily see over her head and hold the reigns at a reasonable distance.

She jerked her head to look into the trees on our left. "Did you hear that?"

I scanned the area, but saw nothing out of the ordinary. "No."

"Never mind then," she said. I kept my eyes peeled for a little longer, but saw nothing out of the ordinary.

I heard a stick snap.

The snow crunched under someone's boot.

"Hold on," I threw a hand up to stop the caravan. Luce looked back at me as I turned the horse in circle to look around. Then I saw them. About eight plague doctor masks peeked out from the trees around us.

"We've got company," I said, staring right at one of the priests. I wasn't confident we could fight them because there were only four of us and only three of us could actually fight. The best option was to kick the horses and run as fast as we could. The priests were all on foot, so we'd probably make it.

"Move, Luce!" I ordered. "Come one! We can outrun them!" Aengel and my horse almost crashed into his before we realized he wasn't moving. "Luce!" I said. "Move!"

He looked forward, only shaking his head.

"Luce! Run!" Aengel cried. Czara was already off her horse and storming over to the ex-priest.

"What are you doing?" she demanded. She smacked his horse's flank to spur him into a canter, but Luce pulled back the reigns before he got anywhere. The priests were surrounding us now, blocking the narrow road or any other escape. The closed in on us, each brandishing a dark metaled sword.

One of them spoke. "Thank you for your cooperation, Brother Ornias. You've been most agreeable."

I think I threw up in my mouth. Rage overtook Czara's features. She stormed towards Luce and pulled him off his horse before any of us realized she was reaching for his leg.

"What. Is. This!"

He laid there in the snow like a complete traitor.

I got off my horse and stood over him next to Czara. Aengel joined us seconds later. I could hardly believe what I was seeing. Luce? Betray us? A democracy seemed more likely. The ocean burning down seemed more likely.

"What have you done?" I said softly. "What have you done?" His face cringed in shame down in the snow.

Czara slammed a leather boot onto his chest, knocking the air out of him.

"Speak."

The priests pulled us away from him before Czara, or I, could smash his face in. Not that Aengel couldn't, she just wouldn't. I shrugged a priest off of me as he grabbed my arm. It took four of them to drag me away, and five of them to contain me. Roaring, I thrashed uncontrollably to get free. When that didn't work, I tried biting my captors. I was forced on the ground, face shoved in the snow.

"Luce! How could you!" I spat through the powder. Aengel was easy for them to control. She was already seizing up from a vision. Czara had sat herself down in the snow to watch the spectacle play out. She never really needed Luce anyways. Maybe she even saw this coming.

I didn't.

He had gotten up and was talking to one of the priests a little bit away from us. His eyes were downcast, and the shame of a thousand sins was radiating from him. I glared at him from the ground, the melting snow soaking my clothes.

I trusted him.

Heck, I had even shared a room with him, I let him save my life, I defended him when Czara picked on him, and I thought we were, well, friends. Apparently not.

He slid the animula from his scabbard and handed it to the priest he was talking to.

"No!" I screamed. "Damn you, Luce!"

"This is ridiculous." Czara stood up, brushing off the snow. "Leather stains," she commented to the closest priest, just before burning a hole in his chest with violet lightning. I took the chance and attacked the priests around me. Between me and Czara, we somehow managed to get all eight down. The blood soaking my clothes was starting to freeze, but I hardly noticed. Stepping over the bodies of the mutilated priests and the red snow, I stormed over to Luce.

He bolted.

He may be fast, but I was faster. I grabbed him by the collar and threw him down in the snow.

"I'm so sorry! I had no other choice! Please, you gotta believe me! I'm so sorry, Eli. I'm so sorry-"

"No, it's my bad. I forgot the part where you changed your name to Satan."

Author's Note

The writing of this book included me revisiting the games my siblings and I played as kids, and several very strange web searches. When I started out writing, my intention was to make a record of the days-long, roleplaying games I grew up with. A lot of my childhood memories are the four of us huddled around the dining room table, maybe some of my big brothers' friends too, going on quests and saving the world with some dice, papers, and our imaginations. Eli, Aengel, and Luce were never characters in our games, but Czara, Mortis, Eli's parents, and the Antimarx were all people I consider childhood friends. Well, maybe not friends, exactly, but I grew up knowing them. Czara was the character my twin sister always played, so I have to say that the two are very much similar. Okay, so they're basically the same person. The werewolf village is another part of the book that was drawn from our games. So really, that's another one of my oldest brother's contributions to the story. Mortis is also my oldest brother's creation, so he gets the credit there too. In truth though, this book turned out to be a story of my own creation, with little Easter eggs hidden throughout the pages for my siblings.

Eli and his mother are knowledgeable about plants and impromptu medicine. I am not. To say the least. So, those moments when Eli had to rely on his past knowledge to save an ailing comrade, I relied on the World Wide Web. Thank you, Speedyremedies.com and Natural-HomeRemedies.org for your help. I felt weird looking up "natural ways to make yourself vomit," but Eli had to get that werewolf blood out somehow.

Other than these things, nothing in this story is based off of any person, place, or thing, living or dead or fiction. So if something looks similar, let's just chalk that one up to two great minds thinking alike.

<u>Special Thanks</u>

It takes a village to raise a child; it took my entire friend circle to get this book published. Thank you, Allie Franks and Trevor Whitby for being my fearless editors. Paige Larson, a thousand thanks for the cover art, and thanks Dan Sweet Jr. for being our male model. This book would not have been possible without you guys. And thanks so much, Colette (Coco) Soulier for making the beautiful website. Al, I want to thank you once more for dealing with my crazy writer shenanigans, the sleepless nights, rants, proof-reading, and all. You're a saint.

About the Author

16 years old when she wrote this, *Ink* is the product of a teenage girl's love for writing and a rampant imagination. Grace loves a good book, some Fair Trade hot chocolate, and her bunny rabbit. She lives in the Greater Boston area with her family, and continues to write, draw, and hang out with her friends.

Ink